IRON COWBOY

**Center Point
Large Print**

**This Large Print Book carries the
Seal of Approval of N.A.V.H.**

IRON COWBOY

Diana Palmer

CENTER POINT PUBLISHING

This Center Point Large Print edition
is published in the year 2008 by arrangement with
Harlequin Books S.A.

The text of this Large Print edition is unabridged. In other
aspects, this book may vary from the original edition.
Printed in the United States of America.
Set in 16-point Times New Roman type.

ISBN: 978-1-60285-160-3

Library of Congress Cataloging-in-Publication Data

Palmer, Diana.
    Iron cowboy / Diana Palmer.--Center Point large print ed.
        p. cm.
    ISBN 978-1-60285-160-3 (lib. bdg. : alk. paper)
    1. Ranchers--Fiction. 2. Texas--Fiction. 3. Large type books. I. Title.

PS3566.A513I76 2008
813'.54--dc22

2008002039

Dear Reader,

I still don't know where this book came from. It was all very mysterious, and I think Tony the Dancer (you'll meet him inside the book) had something to do with it.

I laughed a lot when I saw it unfolding on my computer screen, and I also cried a little along the way. It's not a melancholy book, but, like life itself, it has some heartbreak in it. The hero and heroine are both a bit mysterious. Both have secrets. Both have tragedies in their pasts. As usual, in my eccentric way, I have built false trails, so nothing is quite what it seems at the beginning. I do like surprises, as long as they're nice ones. These are. Trust me.

I hope you enjoy reading *Iron Cowboy* as much as I enjoyed writing it for you.

Love to my fans.

As always, I am your biggest fan,

Diana Palmer

To Ann Painter in Massachusetts with love

IRON COWBOY

One

It was a lovely spring day, the sort of day that makes gentle, green, budding trees and white blossoms look like a spring fantasy has been painted. Sara Dobbs stared out the bookstore's side window wistfully, wishing she could get to the tiny flower bed full of jonquils and buttercups to pick a bouquet for the counter. The flowers were blooming on the street that ran beside the Jacobsville Book Nook, where she worked as assistant manager to Dee Harrison, the owner.

Dee was middle-aged, a small, thin, witty woman who made friends wherever she went. She'd been looking for someone to help her manage the store, and Sara had just lost her bookkeeping position at the small print shop that was going out of business. It was a match made in heaven. Sara spent a good portion of her meager salary on books. She loved to read. Living with her grandfather, a retired college professor, had predisposed her to education. She'd had plenty of time to read when she was with her parents, in one of the most dangerous places on earth.

Sara's father, with her maternal grandfather's assistance, had talked her mother into the overseas work. Her father had died violently. Her mother changed, lost her faith, turned to alcohol. She brought Sara to Jacobsville and moved in with her father. She then launched herself into one scandal after another, using her behavior to punish her father without caring about the cost to her only child. Sara and Grandad had suffered for her blatant immorality. It wasn't until Sara had come home in tears, with bruises all over her, that her mother faced the consequences of what she'd done. The children of one of her mother's lovers had caught her alone in the gym and beaten her bloody. Their father had divorced their mother, who was now facing eviction from their home and the loss of every penny they had; their father had spent it on jewels for Sara's mother.

That had led to worse tragedy. Her mother stopped drinking and seemed to reform. She even went back to church. She seemed very happy, until Sara found her one morning, a few days later . . .

The sound of a vehicle pulling up in the parking lot just in front of the bookstore stopped her painful reveries. At least, she thought, she had a good job and made enough to keep a roof over her head.

Her grandfather's little two-bedroom house outside of town had been left to Sara, along with a small savings account. But there was a mortgage on the house.

She missed the old man. Despite his age, he was young in mind and heart, and adventurous. It was lonely without him, especially since she had no other living family. She had no siblings, no aunts or uncles, or even cousins that she knew about. She had nobody.

The ringing of the electronic bell over the door caught her attention. A tall, grim-looking man came into the small bookstore. He glowered at Sara. He was dressed in an expensive-looking three-piece gray suit and wore hand-tooled black boots and a creamy Stetson. Under the hat was straight, thick, conventionally cut black hair. He had the sort of physique that usually was only seen in motion pictures. But he was no movie star. He looked like a businessman. She glanced out the door and saw a big, black pickup truck with a white horse in a white circle on the truck's door. She knew about the White Horse Ranch outside town. This newcomer, Jared Cameron, had bought it from its previous owner, lock, stock, manager and resident cowboys. Someone said he'd been in town several months earlier for a funeral of some sort, but nobody knew who he was related to that had died. So many old people had out-of-town relatives these days, even in Jacobsville, Texas, a town of less than two thousand inhabitants.

Standing outside next to the driver's side of the black pickup was a tall, husky man with wavy black hair in a ponytail and an olive complexion, wearing a dark suit and sunglasses. He looked like a professional wrestler. He was probably a sort of bodyguard. Maybe his employer had enemies. She wondered why.

The man in the gray suit was glaring at the magazine counter with both hands deep in his pockets, muttering to himself.

Sara wondered what he was looking for. He hadn't asked for assistance, or even looked her way. But the muttering was getting darker by the minute. She couldn't afford to turn away a potential customer. No small town business was that secure.

"May I help you?" she asked with a smile.

He gave her a cold look from pale green eyes in a tanned face that seemed to be all hard lines and angles. His eyes narrowed on her short, straight blond hair, moved over her wide forehead, down over her own green eyes and straight nose and high cheekbones, to her pretty mouth and rounded chin. He made a sound, as if she didn't live up to his specifications. She didn't dare make a comment, but she was really tempted to tell him that if he was shopping for pretty women, a designer boutique in a big city would be a better place to look than a small bookstore.

"You don't carry financial magazines." He made it sound like a hanging offense.

"Nobody around here reads them much," she defended.

His eyes narrowed. "I read them."

She did occasionally have to bite her tongue to save her job. This looked like one of those times. "I'm very sorry. We could order them for you, if you like."

"Forget it. I can subscribe." He glanced toward the mystery paperbacks and scowled again. "I hate paperbacks. Why don't you carry hardcover novels?"

Her tongue was stinging. She cleared her throat. "Well, most of our clientele are working people and they can't afford them."

Both thick black eyebrows arched. "I don't buy paperbacks."

"We can special order any sort of hardcover you want," she said. The smile was wavering, and she was trying hard not to offend him.

He glanced toward the counter at the computer. "Do you have Internet access?"

"Of course." He must think he'd landed in Borneo. She frowned. They probably even had computers in the jungles these days. He seemed to consider Jacobsville, Texas, a holdover from the last century.

"I like mystery novels," he said. "Biographies. I like first-person adventure novels and anything factual on the North African campaign of World War II."

Her heart jumped at the subject he'd mentioned. She cleared her throat. "Would you like all of them at once, then?"

One eyebrow went up. "The customer is always right," he said shortly, as if he thought she was making fun of him.

"Of course he is," she agreed. Her teeth hurt from being clenched in that smile.

"Get me a sheet of paper and a pen. I'll make you a list."

She wouldn't kick him, she wouldn't kick him, she wouldn't kick him . . . She found paper and pencil and handed them to him, still smiling.

He made a list while she answered a phone call. She hung up, and he handed her the list.

She frowned as she read it.

"Now what's wrong?" he asked impatiently.

"I don't read Sanskrit," she began.

He muttered something, took the list back and made minor modifications before handing it back. "It's the twenty-first century. Nobody handwrites anything," he said defensively. "I've got two computers and a PDA and an MP3 player." He gave her a curious look. "Do you know what an MP3 player is?" he asked, just to irritate her.

She reached in her jeans pocket, produced a small iPod Shuffle and earphones. The look that accompanied the action could kill.

"How soon can you get those books here?" he asked.

She could, at least, make out most of the titles with his so-called handwriting corrections. "We order on Mondays," she said. "You'll have as many of these as are in stock at the distributors by next Thursday or Friday."

"The mail doesn't come by horse anymore," he began.

She took a deep breath. "If you don't like small towns, maybe you could go back to wherever you came from. If you can get there by conventional means, that is," with an edge to the smile that accompanied the words.

The insinuation wasn't lost on him. "I'm not the devil."

"Are you sure?" she queried, all wide-eyed.

One eye narrowed. "I'd like these books delivered. I'm usually too busy to make a special trip into town."

"You could send your bodyguard."

He glanced out the door at the big man who was leaning back against the driver's door of the pickup with his arms folded. "Tony the Dancer doesn't run errands."

Her eyes widened more. "Tony the Dancer? Are you in the mob?"

"No, I'm not in the mob!" he growled. "Tony's last name is Danzetta. Tony the Dancer. Get it?"

"Well, he looks like a hit man to me," she returned.

"Known a few of them, have you?" he asked sarcastically.

"If I did, you'd be double-checking your locks tonight," she said under her breath.

"Can you deliver the books?"

"Yes, but it will cost you ten dollars. Gas is expensive."

"What do you drive?" he asked. "A Greyhound bus?"

"I have a VW, thank you very much, but your place is six miles out of town."

"You can tell me the amount when you call to say the books are here. I'll have my accountant cut the check. You can pick it up when you deliver the books."

"All right."

"I'd better give you the number. It's unlisted."

She turned over the sheet of paper with his list of titles on it and copied down the number he gave her.

"I'd also like to get two financial magazines," he added, naming them.

"I'll see if our distributor carries them. He might not."

"Serves me right for moving to Outer Cowpasture," he muttered aloud.

"Well, excuse us for not having malls on every street!" she shot back.

He glowered. "You're the rudest clerk I've seen yet."

"Get your bodyguard to loan you his shades and you won't have to see me at all."

He pursed his lips. "You might get yourself a book on manners."

She smiled sarcastically. "I'll see if I can find one on ogres for you."

His pale eyes swept over her with calculation. "Just the ones I listed, if you please. I'll expect to hear from you late next week."

"Yes, sir."

He cocked his head. "Your boss must have been pretty desperate to leave you in charge of his sole means of support."

"It's a she, not a he. And my boss likes me very much."

"Good thing someone does, I guess." He turned to leave, pausing at the door. "You're wearing two different shades of hose under those slacks, and your earrings don't match."

She had problems with symmetry. Most people knew her background and were kind enough not to mention her lapses. "I'm no slave to popular fashion," she informed him with mock hauteur.

"Yes. I noticed."

He left before she came up with a suitable reply. Lucky for him there wasn't anything expendable that she could have thrown after him.

Dee Harrison rolled in the aisles laughing when she heard Sara's biting description of their new customer.

"It wasn't funny," Sara protested. "He called Jacobsville 'Outer Cowpasture,'" she grumbled.

"Obviously the man has no taste." Dee grinned. "But he did want us to order a lot of books for him, so your sacrifice wasn't in vain, dear."

"But I have to deliver the books to him," she wailed. "He's probably got people-eating dogs and machine guns out there. You should have seen the guy driving him! He looked like a hit man!"

"He's probably just eccentric," Dee said calmingly. "Like old man Dorsey."

She gave her employer a narrow glance. "Old man Dorsey lets his German shepherd sit at the table and eat with him. This guy would probably eat the dog!"

Dee just smiled. A new customer was just what she needed, especially one with expensive tastes in reading. "If he orders a lot of books, you might get a raise," Dee ventured.

Sara just shook her head. Dee didn't understand the situation. If Sara had to be around that particular customer very often, she'd probably end up doing time for assault and battery.

. . .

She went home to her small house. Morris met her at the door. He was an old, battle-scarred yellow tabby cat. Part of his tail was missing, and he had slits in his ears from fights. He'd been a stray who came crying to Sara's back door in a thunderstorm. She'd let him in. That had been eight years ago. Her grandfather had commented that he looked like trouble. Sara defended him.

She never agreed with her grandfather, even after she had to replace a chair and a throw rug that Morris had ripped to shreds. She bought the old cat a scratching post and herself a water pistol. Morris hated water. When he did something he wasn't supposed to, she let him have it. Over the years, he'd calmed down and stopped clawing furniture. Now, he just ate and sprawled in the sun. Occasionally he sat in Sara's lap while she watched her small color television. But he wasn't a cuddling cat, and you couldn't pick him up. He bit.

She stroked him while they watched the latest episode of her favorite forensic show. "I guess it's just as well that we're not overrun with visitors, Morris," she mused softly. "You're definitely an antisocial personality." She pursed her lips as she looked down at him. "I know a guy you'd like," she added on a chuckle. "I must attract animals and people with bad attitudes."

The end of the next week came all too soon. Dee had placed Jared Cameron's order on Monday. Sara was hoping the ogre's order wouldn't come in, allowing her a reprieve to work on her social skills. But all the books in the order arrived like clockwork on Friday.

She phoned the number Jared Cameron had given her.

"Cameron ranch," came a gruff reply.

"Mr. Cameron?" she asked hesitantly, because this didn't sound like the man who'd come into the store earlier.

"He's not here," a gravelly deep voice replied.

She pictured the face that would have gone with that voice, and figured it must be the hit man. "Mr. . . . Danzetta?"

There was a shocked pause. "Yeah. How'd you know?"

"I read minds," she lied.

"No kidding?" He sounded as if he actually believed her.

"Mr. Cameron ordered a lot of books . . ."

"Yeah, he said they were due today. He said for you to bring them out tomorrow about ten. He'll be here."

Tomorrow was Saturday, and she didn't work Saturdays. "Couldn't I leave them with you, and he can send us the check?"

"Tomorrow at ten, he said. He'll be here."

There was no arguing with stone walls. She sighed. "Okay. I'll see him tomorrow."

"Good."

The line went dead. The voice had a decidedly Southern accent. Not a Texas accent. A Georgia one, if she were guessing. She had an ear for accents. Her grandfather had taught students from all over the country and around the world at the Jacobsville Community College, and he often brought them home. Sara had learned a lot about other places.

She put the phone down belatedly. If the bodyguard was part of the mob, it must be the Southern branch. She chuckled. But now she didn't know what to do. Should she call him tomorrow before she started out, to let him know how much he owed? Surely his bookkeeper didn't work weekends.

"You look unsettled," Dee remarked as she started for the front door. "What's wrong?"

"I have to take the ogre's order out to him tomorrow morning."

"On your day off." Dee smiled. "You can have a half day next Wednesday to make up for it. I'll come in at noon and work until closing time."

"You will?" Sara asked, beaming.

"I know how you look forward to your drawing time," Dee replied. "I just know you're going to sell that children's book you're working on. Call Lisa Parks and tell her you'll come next Wednesday to draw her new puppies instead of tomorrow. They'll make a gorgeous page in your story," she added.

Sara grinned. "They're the cutest puppies I've ever seen. Their father was one of the puppies Tom Walker's dog Moose fathered, and their mother is Cy Parks's collie, Bob."

"Bob is a girl dog?" Dee exclaimed.

"Yes. The puppies look like both their parents. Tom asked for one of them. He lost Moose just last month," she added sadly. "They have another dog a little younger than Moose, but Tom loved that old dog. He had him cremated and put in an urn. He's still grieving, though. Lisa e-mailed a picture of the puppies to Tom and said he could have one. He and his oldest daughter went over to pick it out. They'll be ready to go to new homes in a week or so. They're just precious at this age. I'm going to draw them in a big Easter basket."

"You could sell drawings," Dee said.

"I guess so. But I'd never make a living at it," she replied, smiling. "I want to sell books."

"I think you're going to be selling your own books pretty soon," Dee told her. "You have a wonderful talent."

Sara beamed. "Thanks. It's the only thing I inherited from my father. He loved the work he did, but he could draw beautiful portraits." She grimaced. "It was hard, losing him like that."

"Wars are terrible," Dee agreed. "But at least you had your grandfather. He was your biggest fan. He was always bragging about you, to anybody who'd listen."

"I still get letters from Grandad's former students," Sara said. "He taught military history. I guess he had every book ever written on World War II. Especially the campaign in North Africa." She frowned. "Funny, that's what the ogre likes to read about."

"Maybe the ogre is like that lion who got a thorn in his paw, and when the mouse pulled it out, they were friends for life."

Sara glowered at her boss. "No mouse in his right mind would go near that man," she said.

"Except you," came the amused reply.

"Well, I don't have a choice. What do we do about the check?" she asked Dee. "Do I call him before I go over there, or . . ."

Dee picked up the slip of paper with his phone number on it. "I'll call him in the morning. You can put the books in a bag and take them home with you tonight. That way you won't have to come in to town."

"You're sweet, Dee."

The older woman smiled. "So are you." She checked her watch. "I've got to pick Mama up at the beauty parlor and take her home, then I'm going to do paperwork. You know my cell phone number. Call me if you need me."

"I won't, but thanks all the same."

Dee looked uneasy. "You need to have a cell phone, Sara. You can get a prepaid one for next to nothing. I don't like you having to drive home after dark on that dirt road."

"Most of the drug traffickers are in prison now," she reminded her boss.

"That isn't what Cash Grier says," Dee replied. "They locked up the Dominguez woman, and her successor, but there's a man in charge now, and he killed two Mexican policemen at a border crossing, as well

24

as a Border Patrol agent and even a reporter. They say he killed a whole family over near Nuevo Laredo for ratting on him."

"Surely he wouldn't come here," Sara began.

"Drug dealers like it here," Dee returned. "We don't have federal agents—well, except for the DEA agent, Cobb, who works out of Houston and has a ranch here. Our police and sheriff's departments are under-funded and understaffed. That's why that man Lopez tried to set up a distribution network here. They say this new drug lord has property around town that he bought with holding companies, so nobody would know who really owned the land. A farm or ranch way out in the country would be a perfect place to transport drugs to."

"Like they tried once, behind Cy Parks's place and at the old Johnson place."

Dee sighed. "It makes me uneasy, that's all."

"You worry too much," Sara said gently. "Besides, I'm only a mile out of town and I lock all my doors." She looked at the clock on the wall opposite. "You'd better get moving, or your mother's going to be worried about you!"

Dee chuckled. "I guess so. Well, if you need me . . ."

"I'll call."

Dee went out with a wave, leaving Sara alone.

Later in the afternoon, Harley Fowler came in, dusty and sweaty and half out of humor. He pushed his hat back over wet hair.

"What in the world happened to you?" Sara exclaimed. "You look like you've been dragged down a dirt road behind a horse!"

He glowered. "I have."

"Ouch," she sympathized.

"I need a book on Spanish slang. Ranch Spanish slang, if you've got one."

"We have every Spanish dictionary ever published, including slang ones. I'll show you."

She pointed out a rack with dozens of paperback dictionaries, including specific books just on verbs.

"Just the thing," Harley murmured, reading titles. "Mr. Parks still has an account, doesn't he?"

"He and Lisa both do."

"Well, you can put these on his tab." He picked out four and handed them to her.

"Would it be safe to ask why you want them?" she mused as she went behind the counter to the cash register.

"Why not?" he sighed. "I thought I was telling Lanita, Juan's wife, that it was hot outside. She blushed, Juan jumped me, and we rolled around in the dirt until I finally convinced him that I was just talking about the weather. We got up and shook hands, and then he told me what I'd actually said to her. I was just sick." He groaned. "I speak a little Spanish, but I learned it in high school, and I've forgotten how *not* to say embarrassing things." He groaned. "Juan and the rest of the workers speak English, but I thought I might get along better with them if I spoke a little Spanish. And this happens!"

She pursed her lips. "If you want to remark on the weather, in Spanish you say 'there is heat,' not 'I am hot.' Especially in front of a woman."

"Thanks, I do know that now," he replied, soothing his jaw. "That Juan hits like a mule kicking."

"So I've heard."

She totaled the books on the cash register and wrote down the tally in a book of accounts that Dee kept. "We'll bill Mr. Parks."

"Thanks." He took the bag with the books. "If Mr. Parks wants to argue about me buying them, I'll tell him to go talk to Juan."

She grinned. "Good idea."

He smiled back, and hesitated, as if he wanted to say something more. Just then, the phone rang, and it was one of her long-winded customers. She shrugged and waved at Harley. He waved back as he left. She wondered later what he'd been about to say.

He was handsome and well-known in the community for being a hardworking cowboy. He'd actually gone on a mission with three of the town's ex-mercenaries to help stop Manuel Lopez's drug-smuggling operation. He'd earned a lot of respect for his part in it. Sara liked him a lot, but he didn't date much. Rumor was that he'd had a real case on a local girl who'd made fun of his interest in her and threw him over. But he didn't look like a man with a broken heart.

Sara knew about broken hearts. She'd been sweet

on a boy in the community college she attended to learn accounting. So had Marie, her best friend. The boy had dated both of them, but finally started going steady with Marie. A good loser, Sara had been maid of honor at their wedding. Marie and her new husband had moved to Michigan to be near his parents. Sara still wrote to Marie. She was too kindhearted to hold a grudge. Probably, she realized, the boy had only dated her because she was best friends with Marie. She recalled that he spent most of their time together asking her questions about Marie.

She was old-fashioned. Her grandfather had firm opinions about the morality deprived state of modern society. He and Sara went to church regularly and she began to share his views. She wasn't the sort of girl who got invited to wild parties, because she didn't drink or smoke or do drugs. Everyone knew that her grandfather was good friends with one of Police Chief Cash Grier's older patrol officers, too. Her law enforcement connections made the party crowd cautious. It also got around that Sara didn't "give out" on dates. There were too many girls who had no such hang-ups. So Sara and Morris spent most of their Friday and Saturday nights together with Sara's grandfather, watching movies on television.

She wondered where the ogre had gone, and why Tony the Dancer hadn't gone with him. Maybe he was off on a hot date somewhere. She wondered about the sort of woman who might appeal to a man with his gloomy outlook. But then she remembered that he'd been wearing an expensive suit, and driving a new truck, and he owned one of the bigger ranches in the county. Some women wouldn't mind how gloomy and antisocial he was, as long as he had lots of money to spend on them.

He did look like a cold fish. But maybe he was different around people he liked. He'd made it obvious that he didn't like Sara. The feeling was mutual. She hated having to give up her Saturday to his whim.

She phoned Lisa to tell her that she wouldn't be able to come until the following Wednesday.

"That's okay," Lisa replied. "Cy and I wanted to take the baby to the mall in San Antonio on Saturday, but I was going to stay home and wait for you. There's lots of sales on baby clothes and toys."

Like Lisa needed sales, when her husband owned one of the most productive ranches in Texas, she thought, but she didn't say it. "You're always buying that baby clothes," Sara teased. "He's going to be the best-dressed little boy in town."

"We go overboard, I know," Lisa replied, "but we're so happy to have him. Cy and I took a long time to get over losing our first one."

"I remember," Sara said softly. "But birth defects turn up sometimes in the healthiest families, you know. I read about it in one of the medical books we sell. This little boy is going to grow up and be a rancher, just like his parents."

Lisa laughed softly. "Thanks, Sara," she said gently. "You make me feel better every time I talk to you."

"I'll call you Wednesday, okay? Dee's giving me a half-day, so I'll have the afternoon off."

"That will work out fine," Lisa said.

"Thanks."

"You're very welcome."

Sara hung up. Poor Lisa. Her first husband had been killed not long after their wedding. He'd been an undercover DEA agent, whom one of the drug dealer, Lopez's, men had killed. Cy had taken her under his wing and protected her while she waited for the birth of her child. Harley said the baby she was carrying wasn't her husband's, because he had a vasectomy, but she'd thought she was pregnant. Only weeks after marrying Cy, she really was pregnant. But the baby was born with birth defects that were beyond a physician's ability to cure. He'd died when he was only a week old, leaving two devastated parents to grieve. They hadn't rushed into another pregnancy. But this one had worked out without any health issues at all. Their little boy, Gil, was a toddler, and very active.

Sara wondered if she'd ever get married and have a family, but it wasn't something she dwelled on. She was young and the world would have been wide-open for her, except for her one small secret that she wasn't anxious to share with anyone. Still, she was optimistic about the future. Well, except for the ogre.

She sighed. Every life had to have a few little irritations, she decided. And who knew? The ogre might turn out to be a handsome prince inside.

Two

It was pouring rain when Sara reluctantly crawled out of bed the next morning. She looked out the window and sighed.

"Boy, I'd love to go back under the covers and sleep, Morris," she mused as she fed the old cat.

He rubbed up against her pajama-clad legs and purred.

She yawned as she made a pot of coffee and some buttered toast to go with it. Her grandfather had insisted on a balanced breakfast, but Sara couldn't manage a lot of food early in the morning.

She nibbled toast and watched the rain bounce down over the camellia bush next to the window. She was going to get wet.

She dressed in jeans and a cotton blouse and threw her ancient tan raincoat over her clothes. It was embarrassing to wear such a tacky coat to a rich man's house, but it was all she had. Her salary didn't cover many new things. Mostly she shopped at thrift stores. The coat had a stained neck and two or three tears where Sara—never the world's most graceful woman—had tripped over garden stakes or steps or her own feet and brushed against nails and a barbed-wire fence. She looked down and noticed that she was wearing socks that didn't match. Well, it was something she just had to learn to live with. The doctor

31

told her she'd cope. She hoped he was right. She was nineteen, and sometimes she felt fifty when she tried to force her mind to comprehend matching colors.

Groaning, she checked her watch. It was fifteen to ten, and it would take her almost all that time to get to the White Horse Ranch. Well, the ogre would just have to make fun of her. She didn't have time to unload her sock drawer and find mates. They were hidden under her jeans, anyway, and maybe he wouldn't notice.

She stepped right into a hole filled with muddy water getting to her car. Her sneakers and her socks were immediately soaked. She groaned again as she unlocked the little car and quickly climbed in. The seats were leather, thank goodness, and they'd shed water. Her VW was seven years old, but the mechanics at Turkey Sanders's used car lot kept it in good repair. Despite his reputation for bad car sales, Turkey prided himself on his mechanics.

She patted its cracked dash. The VW had been wrecked, so she got it very cheaply. Probably it would fall apart if she tried to drive it as far as San Antonio. But she never left the Jacobsville area, and it was dependable transportation.

It started on the first go, making that lovely race car sound that made her think of luxury racers as she gunned the engine. If she closed her eyes and did that, sometimes it sounded just like a Formula 1 challenge car.

"In my dreams," she laughed to herself. She

wouldn't earn enough in her lifetime to make six months of payments on one of those fancy sports cars. But it was just as well. The little black VW suited her very well.

She pulled out of her driveway onto the dirt road that led out to the state highway. It had been recently scraped and a little new gravel had been laid down, but it was still slippery in the rain. She gritted her teeth as she felt the car slide around in the wet mud. At least it was flat land, and even if she did go into a ditch, it wouldn't be a deep one. All the same, she didn't look forward to walking for help in that molasses-thick mud. She remembered a long walk in similar red mud, overseas, with the sound of guns echoing . . . She drew her mind back to the present. Dwelling on the past solved nothing.

By downshifting, not hitting the brakes and going slowly, she managed to get to the paved highway. But she was going to be late getting to the ogre's house. She grimaced. Well, it couldn't be helped. She'd just have to tell him the truth and hope he was under-standing about it.

"I specifically said ten o'clock," he shot at her when he opened the front door.

He was wearing jeans and a chambray shirt and working boots—you could tell by the misshapen con-tours of them that many soakings had caused—and a ratty black Stetson pulled low over his forehead. Even in working garb, he managed to look elegant.

He looked like a cowboy, but they could have used him as a model for one made of metal. An iron cowboy.

She had to fight a laugh at the comparison.

"And you're dripping wet all over," he muttered, glaring at her clothes. "What the hell did you do, swim through mud holes on your way here?"

"I stepped in a mud puddle on the way to my car," she began, clutching a plastic bag that held his books.

He looked past her. "I don't know what the hell that thing is, but I wouldn't dignify it by calling it a car."

Her eyes began to glitter. "Here," she said, thrusting the books at him.

"And your manners could use some work," he added bitingly.

" 'Cast not your pearls before swine!' " she quoted angrily.

Both eyebrows went up under the hat. "If that raincoat is any indication of your finances, you'd be lucky to be able to toss a cultured pearl at a pig. Which I am not one of," he added firmly.

"My boss said she'd call you . . ."

"She did." He took a folded check out of his shirt pocket and handed it to her. "Next time I order books, I'll expect you at the stated time. I'm too busy to sit in the house waiting for people to show up."

"The road I live on is six inches thick in wet mud," she began.

"You could have phoned on the way and told me that," he retorted.

"With what, smoke signals?" she asked sourly. "I don't have a cell phone."

"Why am I not surprised?" he asked with pure sarcasm.

"And my finances are none of your business!"

He glanced down. "If they were, I'd quit. No accountant is going to work for a woman who can't afford two matching socks."

"I have another pair just like this one at home!"

He frowned. He leaned closer. "What in the world is *that?*" he asked, indicating her left sleeve.

She looked down. "Aahhhhhh!" she screamed, jumping from one leg to the other. "Get it off, get it off! Aaaahhhh!"

The large man in the house came out onto the porch, frowning. When he followed his employer's pointed finger, he spotted the source of the uproar. "Oh," he said.

He walked forward, caught Sara's arm with a big hand, picked up the yellow hornet on her sleeve, slammed it to the porch and stepped on it with a shoe the size of a shoebox.

"It's just a hornet," Mr. Danzetta said gently.

Sara stared down at the smashed insect and drew in a deep breath. "It's a yellow hornet. I got stung by one of them once, on my neck. It swelled up and I had to be taken to the emergency room. I've been scared of them ever since." She smiled up at him. "Thank you." Odd, she thought, how familiar he looked. But she was almost certain she'd never seen him before. Her condition made it difficult for her to remember the past.

The ogre glared at his employee, who was smiling at Sara and watching her with something like recognition. He noted the glare, cleared his throat and went back into the house.

"Don't start flirting with the hired help," he told her firmly after the front door had closed behind Tony.

"I said thank you! How can you call that flirting?" she asked, aghast.

"I'll call the store when I need a new supply of books," he replied, ignoring her question.

She read quickly herself, but he had eight books there. But he might not be reading them, she thought wickedly. He might be using them for other purposes: as doorstops, maybe.

"You brought the books. I gave you a check. Was there something else?" he asked with a cold smile. "If you're lonely and need companionship, there are services that advertise on television late at night," he added helpfully.

She drew herself up to her full height. "If I were lonely, this is the last place in the world that I'd look for relief!" she informed him.

"Then why are you still here?"

She wouldn't kick him, she wouldn't kick him . . .

"And don't spin out going down my driveway," he called after her. "That's new gravel!"

She hoped he was watching her the whole way. She dislodged enough gravel to cover a flower bed on her way down the driveway.

• • •

It was a long, wet weekend. She knew that nobody around Jacobs County would be complaining about the rain. It was a dry, unusually hot spring. She read in the market bulletins online that ranchers were going to pay high prices for corn. Floods in the Midwest and Great Plains were killing the corn there, and drought was getting it in the South and Southwest. Considering the vast amounts of the grain that were being used as biofuel, and the correspondingly higher prices it was commanding, it looked as if some small ranchers and farmers might go broke because they couldn't afford to feed it to their cattle. Not to mention the expense of running farm machinery, which mostly burned gasoline.

She was glad she wasn't a farmer or rancher. She did feel sorry for the handful of small ranchers around town. One day, she thought, there would be no more family agriculture in the country. Everything would be owned by international corporations, using patented seed and genetically enhanced produce. It was a good thing that some small farmers were holding on to genetically pure seeds, raising organic crops. One day, the agricultural community might be grateful, if there was ever a wholesale dying out of the genetically modified plants.

"Well, you're deep in thought, aren't you?" Dee teased as she walked in the door the following Wednesday, just before noon.

Sara blinked, startled by her boss's appearance.

"Sorry," she said, laughing. "I was thinking about corn."

Dee stared at her. "OOOOOkay," she drawled.

"No, I'm not going mad," Sara chuckled. "I read an article in this farm life magazine." She showed it to the older woman. "It's about the high prices corn is going to get this year."

Dee shook her head. "I don't know what the smaller ranchers are going to do," she said. "Gas prices are so high that it's hard to afford enough fuel to run tractors and trucks, and now they'll have to hope the hay crop is good or they'll have to sell off cattle before winter rather than having to feed them stored corn." She sighed. "I expect even the Ballengers will be feeling a pinch, with their feedlot."

"It must be tough, having your livelihood depend on the weather," she remarked.

"Yes, it is. I grew up on a little truck farm north of here," Dee told her. "One year, we had a drought so bad that everything we grew died. Dad had to borrow on the next year's profits to buy seed and fertilizer." She shook her head. "Finally he couldn't deal with the uncertainty anymore. He got a job fixing engines at one of the car dealerships."

"It's so bad, you know—floods in the Midwest and drought here and in the Southeast. Too much water or not enough. They need to build aqueducts like the Romans did and share that water with places that need it."

"Not a bad idea, but who'd pay for it?"

Sara laughed. "I don't guess anybody could. But it was a nice thought."

Dee checked her watch. "You'd better get a move on, before we get swamped with customers and you're late leaving."

"I'll do that. Thanks, Dee."

The older woman smiled. "Good luck with those drawings."

Lisa Parks had blond hair and a sweet smile. She was carrying Gil, her eighteen-month-old toddler, when she came to the door to let Sara in. The baby had brownish colored hair and his eyes were green, like his father's. He was wearing a two-piece sailor suit.

"Doesn't he look cute!" Sara enthused over the little boy, while Lisa beamed.

"Our pride and joy," Lisa murmured, kissing the child on his soft nose. "Come in."

Sara stepped into the cool confines of the house. It had been a bachelor house for years, but Lisa's feminine touches made it into a home.

"Want coffee before you start?" Lisa asked, shifting Gil on her hip while he chanted happy noises.

"After, if you don't mind," came the smiling reply. "I always try to avoid work if it's at all possible."

"Don't we all? I've got the puppies out in the barn." She led the way down the back steps, pausing at the sound of a horse approaching. Gil was still making happy baby sounds, cradled on his mother's hip.

Harley Fowler was just riding into the yard. He

spotted Sara with Lisa and smiled hugely. "Hi, Sara."

"Hello, Harley. How's the Spanish coming along?"

He glanced at Lisa, who grinned at him. He shrugged. "Well, I guess I'm learning some. But Juan is a better teacher than any book."

"How's your jaw?" Sara asked with twinkling eyes.

He fingered it. "Much better." He smiled back.

"Uh oh, Mama," Gil said, frowning. "Uh oh." He squirmed.

"Uh oh means somebody needs a diaper change," Lisa laughed. She glanced at Harley and, sensing something, concealed a smile. "Harley, if you've got a minute, would you mind showing Sara the pups while I change Gil? We're working on potty training, but it's early days yet," she added on a laugh.

Harley beamed. "I'd be happy to!" He climbed down gracefully out of the saddle and held the reins, waiting for Sara. "Are you going to adopt one of the puppies?"

She blinked. "Well, I hadn't thought about that. I have a cat, you know, and he really doesn't like dogs much. I think one tried to eat him when he was younger. He's got scars everywhere and even dogs barking on television upsets him."

He frowned. "But you came to see the puppies . . . ?"

She showed him her drawing pad. "I came to sketch the puppies," she corrected, "for the children's book I'm writing."

"Someday she's going to be famous, and we can all say we knew her back when," Lisa teased. "I'll have coffee ready when you're done, Sara. I made a pound cake, too."

"Thanks," Sara called after her.

Lisa waved as she took the baby back into the house.

Harley tied his horse to the corral fence and walked into the dim confines of the barn with Sara. In a stall filled with fresh hay were five puppies and Bob the Collie. She was nursing the babies. In the stall beside hers was Puppy Dog, Lisa's dog, no longer a puppy. He looked exactly like Tom Walker's dog, Moose.

"A girl dog named Bob," Sara mused.

"Boss said if Johnny Cash could have a boy named 'Sue,' he could have a girl dog named Bob."

"She's so pretty," Sara said. "And the puppies are just precious!"

"Three males, two females," he said. "Tom's got first choice, since they're Moose's grandkids." He shook his head. "He's taking Moose's loss hard. He loved that old dog, even though he was a disaster in the house."

"Moose saved Tom's daughter from a rattler," Sara reminded him. "He was a real hero."

"You want a chair?" he asked.

"This old stool will do fine. Thanks anyway." She pulled up the rickety stool, opened her pad and took her pencils out of her hip pocket.

"Will it make you nervous if I watch?"

She grinned up at him. "Of course not."

He lolled against the stall wall and folded his arms,

concentrating on the way her hand flew over the page, the pencil quickly bringing the puppies to life on the off-white sheet. "You're really good," he said, surprised.

"Only thing I was ever good at in school," she murmured while she drew. She was also noting the pattern of colors on the pups and shading her drawing to match. Then she wrote down the colors, so she wouldn't forget them when she started doing the illustrations for her book in pastels.

"I can fix anything mechanical," he said, "but I can't draw a straight line."

"We all have our talents, Harley," she said. "It wouldn't do for all of us to be good at the same thing."

"No, it wouldn't, I guess."

She sketched some more in a personable silence.

"I wanted to ask you in the bookstore, but we got interrupted," he began. "There's going to be a concert at the high school this Saturday. They're hosting a performance by the San Antonio Symphony Orchestra. I wondered if, well, if you'd like to go. With me," he added.

She looked up, her soft eyes smiling. "Well, yes, I would," she said. "I'd thought about it, because they're doing Debussy, and he's my favorite composer. But I didn't have the nerve to go by myself."

He chuckled, encouraged. "Then it's a date. We could leave earlier and have supper at the Chinese place. If you like Chinese?"

"I love it. Thanks."

"Then I'll pick you up about five on Saturday. Okay?"

She smiled at him. He was really nice. "Okay."

He glanced out of the barn at his horse, which was getting restless. "I'd better get back out to the pasture. We're dipping cattle and the vet's checking them over. I'll see you Saturday."

"Thanks, Harley."

"Thank *you*."

She watched him walk away. He was good-looking, local and pleasant to be around. What a difference from that complaining, bad-tempered rancher who hadn't even sympathized with her when she'd almost drowned delivering his stupid books!

Now why had she thought about Jared Cameron? She forced herself to concentrate on the puppies.

Harley picked her up at five on Saturday in his aged, but clean, red pickup truck. He was wearing a suit, and he looked pretty good. Sara wore a simple black dress with her mother's pearls and scuffed black high-heeled shoes that she hoped wouldn't be noticed. She draped a lacy black mantilla around her shoulders.

"You look very nice," Harley said. "I figure there will be people there in jeans and shorts, but I always feel you should dress up to go to a fancy concert."

"So do I," she agreed. "At least it isn't raining," she added.

"I wish it would," he replied. "That nice shower we got last Saturday is long gone, and the crops are suffering. We're still in drought conditions."

"Don't mention that shower," she muttered. "I was out in it, sliding all over Jeff Bridges Road in my VW, bogged up to my knees in mud, just to deliver Jared Cameron's books!"

He glanced at her. "Why didn't he go to the store and get them himself?"

"He's very busy."

He burst out laughing. "Hell! Everyone's very busy. He could spare thirty minutes to drive into town. God knows, he's got half a dozen cars. That big fella who works for him is something of a mechanic in his spare time. He keeps the fleet on the road."

"What sort of cars?" she asked curiously.

"There's a sixties Rolls-Royce Silver Shadow, a thirties Studebaker and several assorted sports cars, mostly classics. He collects old cars and refurbishes them."

"He arrived at our store in a truck," she said flatly.

"From time to time that big fella wearing fancy suits drives him around."

"Do you know where he came from?"

Harley shook his head. "Somebody said he was from Montana, but I'm not sure. He came here for a funeral about eight months ago. Nobody can remember whose."

"A relative, you think?"

He shrugged. "It was at one of the old country churches. Mount Hebron Baptist, I think."

"That's where I go to church," she said, frowning. "Grandad's buried there. But I don't remember reading about any funeral in the bulletin for out-of-town people."

"It was a private service, they said. Just ashes, not even a coffin."

She pursed her lips and whistled softly. "I wouldn't like to be burned."

"I would," he said, grinning at her. "A true Viking's funeral. Nothing wrong with that. Then they can put you in a nice-looking urn and set you on the mantel above the fireplace. Nice and neat. No upkeep."

She laughed. "Harley, you're terrible!"

"Yes, but I do have saving graces. I can whistle and carry a tune. Oh, and I can gather eggs. Just ask the boss's wife!"

They had a nice meal at the local Chinese restaurant and then Harley drove them to the high school. There were a lot of people on hand for the rare big city musical talent. Both Ballengers and their wives and teenaged kids, and a few of the Tremaynes and two Hart brothers and their families.

Harley caught Sara's arm gently to help her up onto the sidewalk from the parking lot, and then let his fingers accidentally catch in hers. She didn't object. She'd always liked Harley. It was nice, to have a man find her attractive, even if it was just in a friendly way.

He was smiling down at her when they almost collided with a man in line. The man, nicely dressed in a suit and a wide-brimmed top-of-the-line John B. Stetson cowboy hat, turned his head back toward them and green eyes glared belligerently.

"Sorry, Mr. Cameron," Harley said at once.

Jared Cameron gave them both a speaking glance and turned his attention back to the line, which was rapidly moving inside. When he was out of earshot, Sara muttered, "He ran into us. You didn't have to apologize."

He chuckled. "It isn't the place for a skirmish, you know," he teased.

She grimaced. "Sorry, Harley. I don't like him, that's all. He's too full of himself."

"He's just bought that huge ranch," he reminded her. "He must live on a higher level than most of us. I guess he thinks he's above normal courtesies."

She only nodded. She hadn't liked the antagonism in the tall man's eyes when he'd looked at Harley.

They got their tickets and found seats as far away from Jared Cameron as Sara could possibly manage. Then she lost herself in the beautiful musical landscapes created by the themes of Claude Debussy. Harley seemed to enjoy the concert as much as she did. It was nice to have something in common.

On the way out, they noticed Jared Cameron speaking earnestly with Police Chief Cash Grier, who'd shown up just after the concert began and stood at the back of the room. Sara wondered what they were talking about. But it was none of her business.

It was ten o'clock when Harley dropped her off at her home. She smiled up at him. "Thanks, Harley. I had a really nice time."

"So did I. Want to go to a movie next Friday?"

Her heart jumped pleasantly. He liked her! She beamed. "Yes. I would."

He chuckled. "That's great!"

He hesitated. So did she. Her experience of men was extremely limited. Her upbringing had been strict and unrelenting on the issue of morals. Her past wasn't widely known around Jacobsville, but her reputation was rock-solid. It was why she hadn't dated much. Harley knew that. But it didn't seem to bother him overmuch. After a minute's deliberation, he bent and brushed his mouth briefly, softly over hers. "Good night, Sara."

She smiled. "Good night, Harley."

He jumped back into the truck, waved and took off down the driveway.

She watched the truck disappear into the distance, frowning as she considered that brief kiss. It hadn't touched her. She liked Harley. She'd have loved having a steady boyfriend, just for the novelty of the thing. But she hadn't felt anything when he kissed her. Maybe you just had to work up to those feelings, she told herself as she unlocked her door and went inside. It was early days in their relationship. They had plenty of time to experiment.

It was the week after the concert before her nemesis placed another order. This time he did it on the telephone, and to Dee, who got to the telephone first early Monday morning.

"What a selection," Dee exclaimed when she hung up. She read down the list, shaking her head. "Greek and Roman writers of the classics, some science fiction, two books on drug interdiction and two on South American politics. Oh, and one on independent contractors. Mercenaries."

"Maybe he's thinking of starting a war," Sara offered. "In some other country, of course." She pursed her lips and her eyes twinkled. "Maybe he's anxious to skip town because he's so fascinated by me!"

Dee looked at her over her glasses. "Excuse me?"

"It's just a theory I'm working on," she said facetiously. "I mean, I'm growing into a femme fatale. Harley Fowler can't resist me. What if my fatal charm has worked its magic on Mr. Cameron and he's running scared? He might feel a need to escape before he gets addicted to me!"

"Sara, do you feel all right?"

Sara just grinned. "I never felt better."

"If you say so. I'll get these ordered." She glanced at Sara. "He wants you to take them out to him on Saturday."

Sara grimaced. "He just likes ruining my week-ends."

"He hardly knows you, dear. I'm sure it's not that."

Sara didn't answer her.

On Thursday, Harley phoned with bad news. "I have to fly to Denver on business for the boss, and I'll be gone a week or more," he said miserably. "So we can't go to the movies on Friday."

"That's all right, Harley," she assured him. "There will be a movie left when you get back that we can go see. Honest."

He laughed. "You make everything so easy, Sara."

"You have a safe trip."

"I'll do my best. Take care."

"You, too."

She hung up and wondered idly why Harley had to go out of town just before they went on another date. It was as if fate was working against her. She'd looked forward to it, too. Now all she had to antici-pate was delivering books to the ogre. It wasn't a happy thought. Not at all.

Well, she told herself, it could always be worse. She could be dating HIM—the ogre.

Three

Sara took the ogre's books home with her on Friday, just as she had the last time, so that she didn't have to go to town. At least it wasn't pouring rain when she went out to her car early Saturday morning to make the drive to the White Horse Ranch.

This time, he was waiting for her on the porch. He was leaning against one of the posts with his hands in his jean pockets. Like last time, he was wearing working garb. Same disreputable boots and hat, same unpleasant expression. Sara tried not to notice what an incredible physique he had, or how handsome he was. It wouldn't do to let him know how attractive she found him.

He looked pointedly at his watch as she came up the steps. "Five minutes late," he remarked.

Her eyebrows arched. "I am not," she shot back. "My watch says ten, exactly."

"My watch is better than yours," he countered.

"I guess so, if you judge it by the amount of gold on the band instead of the mechanics inside it," she retorted.

"You're testy for a concert goer," he returned. He smiled, and it wasn't sarcastic. "You like Debussy, do you?"

"Yes."

"Who else?"

She was taken aback by the question. "I like

Resphigi, Rachmaninoff, Haydn and some modern composers like the late Basil Poledouris and Jerry Goldsmith. I also like James Horner, Danny Elfman, Harry Gregson-Williams and James Newton Howard."

He eyed her curiously. "I thought a country girl like you would prefer fiddles to violins."

"Well, even here in Outer Cowpasture, we know what culture is," she countered.

He chuckled deeply. "I stand corrected. What came in?" he asked, nodding toward the books she was carrying.

She handed the bag to him. He looked over the titles, nodding and pulled a check out of his pocket, handing it to her.

"Is it serious?" he asked abruptly.

She just stared at him. "Is what serious?"

"You and the cowboy at the concert. What's his name, Fowler?"

"Harley Fowler. We're friends."

"Just friends?"

"Listen, I've already been asked that question nine times this week. Just because I go out with a man, it doesn't mean I'm ready to have his children."

Something touched his eyes and made them cold. His faintly friendly air went into eclipse. "Thanks for bringing the books out," he said abruptly. He turned and went in the house without another word, closing the door firmly behind him.

Sara went back to her car, dumbfounded. She

couldn't imagine what she'd said to make him turn off like a blown lightbulb.

The next day she went to church and then treated herself to a nice lunch at Barbara's Café in town. The ogre's odd behavior had disturbed her. She couldn't understand what she'd said to put that look on his lean face. She was upset because she didn't understand. She wasn't a woman who went around trying to hurt other people, even when they deserved it.

After lunch, on an impulse she drove back to her church, parked her car and walked out into the cemetery. She wanted to see her grandfather's grave and make sure the silk flowers she'd put there for Father's Day—today—were still in place. Sometimes the wind blew them around. She liked talking to him as well; catching him up on all the latest news around town. It would probably look as if she were crazy if anyone overheard her. But she didn't care. If she wanted to think her grandfather could hear her at his grave, that was nobody else's business.

She paused at his headstone and stooped down to remove a weed that was trying to grow just beside the tombstone. Her grandmother was buried beside him, but Sara had never known her. She'd been a very small child when she died.

She patted the tombstone. "Hello, Grandad," she said softly. "I hope you're in a happy place with Granny. I sure do miss you. Especially in the summer. Remember how much fun we had going fishing together? You caught that big bass the last time, and fell in the river trying to get him reeled in." She laughed softly. "You said he was the tastiest fish you'd ever eaten."

She tugged at another weed. "There's this new guy in town. You'd like him. He loves to read and he owns a big ranch. He's sort of like an ogre, though. Very antisocial. He thinks I look like a bag lady . . ."

She stopped talking when she realized she wasn't alone in the cemetery. Toward the far corner, a familiar figure was tugging weeds away from a tombstone, patting it with his hand. Talking to it. She hadn't even heard him drive up.

Without thinking of the consequences, she went toward him. Here, among the tombstones, there was no thought of causing trouble. It was a place people came to remember, to honor their dead.

She stopped just behind him and read the tombstone. "Ellen Marist Cameron," it said. She would have been nine years old, today.

He felt her there and turned. His eyes were cold, full of pain, full of hurt.

"Your daughter," she guessed softly.

"Killed in a wreck," he replied tonelessly. "She'd gone to the zoo with a girlfriend and her parents. On the way back, a drunk driver crossed the median and t-boned them on the side my daughter was occupying. She died instantly."

"I'm sorry."

He cocked his head. "Why are you here?"

"I come to talk to my grandad," she confessed, avoiding his eyes. "He died recently of a massive coronary. He was all the family I had left."

He nodded slowly. "She—" he indicated the tombstone "—was all the family I had left. My parents are long dead. My wife died of a drug overdose a week after Ellen was killed." He looked out across the crop of tombstones with blank eyes. "My grandfather used to live here. I thought it was a good place to put her, next to him."

So that was the funeral he'd come here to attend. His child. No wonder he was bitter. "What was she like?" she asked.

He looked down at her curiously. "Most people try to avoid the subject. They know it's painful, so they say nothing."

"It hurts more not to talk about them," she said simply. "I miss my grandfather every day. He was my best friend. He taught history at the local college. We went fishing together on weekends."

"She liked to swim," he said, indicating the tombstone. "She was on a swim team at her elementary school. She was a whiz at computers," he added, laughing softly. "I'd be floundering around trying to find a Web site, and she'd make two keystrokes and bring it up on the screen. She was . . . a child . . . of great promise." His voice broke.

Without counting the cost, Sara stepped right up against him and put her arms around him. She held on tight.

She felt the shock run through him. He hesitated, but only for a minute. His own arms slid around her. He held her close while the wind blew around them, through the tall trees that lined the country cemetery. It was like being alone in the world. Tony Danzetta was out of sight watching, of course, even if he couldn't be seen. Jared couldn't be out of his sight, even at a time like this.

He let out a long breath, and some of the tension seemed to drain out of him. "I couldn't talk about her. There's a hole in my life so deep that nothing fills it. She was my world, and while she was growing up, I was working myself to death making money. I never had time to go to those swim meets, or take her places on holidays. I wasn't even there last Christmas, because I was working a deal in South America and I had to fly to Argentina to close it. She was supposed to spend Christmas with me. She had Thanksgiving with her mother." He drew in a ragged breath and his arms involuntarily contracted around Sara's slim figure. "She never complained. She was happy with whatever time I could spare for her. I wish I'd done more. I never thought we'd run out of time. Not this soon."

"Nobody is ever ready for death," Sara said, eyes closed as she listened to the steady, reassuring heartbeat under her ear. "I knew Grandad was getting old, but I didn't want to see it. So I pretended everything was fine. I lost my parents years ago. Grandad and I were the only family left."

She felt him nodding.

"Did she look like you?" she asked.

"She had my coloring. But she had her mother's hair. She wasn't pretty, but she made people feel good just being around her. She thought she was ugly. I was always trying to explain to her that beauty isn't as important as character and personality."

There was a long, quiet, warm silence.

"Why did you decide to live here?" she asked suddenly.

He hesitated. "It was a business decision," he replied, withdrawing into himself. "I thought new surroundings might help."

She pulled back and his arms fell away from her. She felt oddly chilled. "Does it help?"

He searched her eyes quietly. After a minute, the intensity of the look brought a flaming blush to her cheeks and she looked down abruptly.

He laughed softly at her embarrassment. "You're bashful."

"I am not. It's just hot," she protested, putting a little more distance between them. Her heart was racing and she felt oddly hot. That wouldn't do at all. She didn't dare show weakness to the enemy.

"It wasn't an insult," he said after a minute. "There's nothing wrong with being shy." His eyes narrowed. "Who looks after you, if you get sick? Your boss?"

"Dee's wonderful, but she's not responsible for me.

I look out for myself." She glanced at him. "How about you?"

He shrugged. "If it looked like I was dying, Tony the Dancer would probably call somebody if he was around—if he wasn't on holiday or having days off. My lawyer might send a doctor out, if it was serious and somebody called."

"But would they take care of you?" she persisted.

"That's not their job."

She drew in a long breath. "I know you don't like me. But maybe we could look out for each other."

His dark eyebrows lifted. "Be each other's family, in other words."

"No ties," she said at once. "We'd just be there if one of us was sick."

He seemed to be seriously considering it. "I had flu and almost died last winter," he said quietly. "It was just after I lost my daughter. If Tony hadn't come back early from Christmas holidays, I guess I'd have died. It went into pneumonia and I was too sick and weak to get help."

"Something like that happened to me this year," she said. "I got sick and I had this horrible pain in my stomach. I stayed in bed for days until I could get up and go back to work. It was probably just the stomach bug that was going around, but I thought, what if it was something serious? I couldn't even get to the phone."

He nodded. "I've had the same thoughts. Okay. Suppose we do that?"

She smiled. "It's not such a bad idea, is it?"

"Not bad at all."

"I would be more amenable to the plan if you'd stop treating me like a bag lady," she added.

"Stop dressing like one," he suggested.

She glowered up at him. "I am not dressed like a bag lady."

"Your socks never match. Your jeans look like they've been worn by a grizzly bear. Your T-shirts all have pictures or writing on them."

"When you're working, you don't look all that tidy yourself," she countered, not comfortable with telling him the truth about her odd apparel, "and I wouldn't dare ask what you got on your boots to make them smell so bad."

His eyes began to twinkle. "Want to know? It was," and he gave her the vernacular for it so wickedly that she blushed.

"You're a bad man."

He studied her closely. "If you want to be my family, you have to stop saying unkind things to me. Give a dog a bad name," he said suggestively.

"I'd have to work on that," she replied.

He drew in a long breath as he glanced back at the small grave. "Why did you come out here today?"

She smiled sadly. "Today is Father's Day. I put some new silk flowers on Grandad's grave. Sometimes the wind blows them away. I wanted to make sure they were still there."

"I meant to call one of the local florists and get

them to come out and put a fresh bouquet on her grave. But I've had some business problems lately," he added without specifying what they were. "I write myself notes about things like that." He smiled wryly. "Then I misplace the notes."

"I do that all the time," she confessed.

He cocked his head, staring at her. "Why can't you wear things that match?" he asked, noting that she had on mismatched earrings.

She grimaced. It was much too early in their ambiguous relationship to tell him the real reason. She lied instead. "I'm always in a hurry. I just put on whatever comes to hand. Around town, people know I do it and nobody makes fun of me." She hesitated. "That's not quite true. When I came here to live with Grandad, some of the local kids made it hard on me."

"Why?"

"Well, my mother wasn't exactly pure as the driven snow," she confessed. "She had affairs with three or four local men, and broke up marriages. The children of those divorces couldn't get to her, but I was handy."

She said it matter-of-factly, without blame. He scowled. "You should sound bitter, shouldn't you?" he queried.

She smiled up at him. "Giving back what you get sounds good, but these days you can end up in jail for fighting at school. I didn't want to cause Grandad any more pain than Mom already had. You see, he was a college professor, very conservative. What she did embarrassed and humiliated him. One of her lovers was his department head at college. She did it deliberately. She hated Grandad."

His eyes narrowed. "Can I ask why?"

That was another question she didn't feel comfortable answering. Her eyes lowered to his tie. "I'm not really sure," she prevaricated.

He knew she was holding something back. Her body language was blatant. He wondered if she realized it.

Another question presented itself. He frowned. "Just how old are you?"

She looked up, grinning. "I'm not telling."

He pursed his lips, considering. "You haven't lost your illusions about life, yet," he mused, noting the odd flicker of her eyelids when he said it. "I'd say you haven't hit your mid-twenties yet, but you're close."

He'd missed it, but she didn't let on. "You're not bad," she lied.

He stuck his hands in the pockets of his slacks and looked at the sky. "No rain yet. Probably none for another week, the meteorologists say," he remarked. "We need it badly."

"I know. We used to have this old guy, Elmer Randall, who worked at the newspaper office helping to run the presses. He was part Comanche. Every time we had a drought, he'd get into his tribal clothes and go out and do ceremonies outside town."

"Did it work?" he asked with real interest.

She laughed. "One time after he did it, we had a flood. It almost always rained. Nobody could figure it out. He said his grandfather had been a powerful shaman and rode with Quanah Parker." She shrugged. "People believe what they want to, but I thought he might really have a gift. Certainly, nobody told him to stop."

"Whatever works," he agreed. He checked his watch. "I'd better get home. I'm expecting a phone call from Japan."

"Do you speak the language?"

He laughed. "I try to. But the company I'm merging with has plenty of translators."

"I'll bet Japan is an interesting place," she said with dreamy eyes. "I've never been to Asia in my whole life."

He looked surprised. "I thought everybody traveled these days."

"We never had the money," she said simply. "Grandad's idea of international travel was to buy Fodor's Guides to the countries that interested him. He spent his spare cash on books, hundreds of books."

"He taught history, you said. What was his period?"

She hesitated as she looked up at his lean, handsome face. Wouldn't it sound too pat and coincidental to tell him the truth?

He frowned. "Well?"

She grimaced. "World War II," she confessed. "The North African theater of war."

His intake of breath was audible. "You didn't mention that when I ordered books on the subject."

"I thought it would sound odd," she said. "I mean, here you were, a total stranger looking for books on that subject, and my grandfather taught it. It seems like some weird coincidence."

"Yes, but they do happen." He moved restlessly. "Did he have autobiographies?"

"Yes, all sorts of first person accounts on both sides of the battle. His favorite subjects were German Field Marshal Erwin Rommel and General George Patton, but he liked the point of view of the 9th Australian Division, as well as British General Bernard Montgomery's memoirs."

"I asked the high school age son of one of my vice presidents which of the generals he liked to read about when he was studying history. He said they hadn't taught him about any individual officers. He didn't even know who Rommel was."

The allusion to vice presidents went right by her. She smiled sheepishly. She'd only graduated from high school two years before, and he didn't know that. "I didn't, either, from high school courses," she confessed. "But Grandad was good for a two-hour lecture on any subject I mentioned."

He pursed his lips, really interested. "Who was the last commander of the British Eighth Army before Montgomery in North Africa?"

She chuckled. "You don't think I know, do you? It was Auchinleck—Sir Claude. He was a big, redheaded man, and his wife was from America."

His eyebrows arched. "You're good. What was Rommel's wife called?"

"Her name was Lucie, but he called her Lu. They had a son, Manfred, who eventually became Lord Mayor of Stuttgart, Germany." She wiggled her eyebrows at him. "Want to know what sort of anti-tank field artillery Rommel used that confounded the British generals? It was the 88 millimeter antiaircraft gun. He camouflaged them and then lured the British tanks within firing range. They thought it was some sort of super weapon, but they were just regular anti-aircraft weapons. One captured officer told Rommel that it wasn't fair to use them against tanks. But it was war."

"It was." He was looking at her in a totally different way than he had before. "Do you ever loan books?"

She frowned. "Well, I never have before. But I might make an exception for you. Grandad would have loved talking with you about North Africa."

"I would have enjoyed it, too." He glanced again at his watch. "Lord, I'm late!"

"I have to get back home, too." She looked down at the tombstone. "I'm sorry about your daughter."

He sobered. "I'm sorry about your grandfather. Holidays are the worst times, aren't they? I stayed drunk for two days last Christmas. It was my first without her."

"I don't drink," she replied. "But my heart wasn't in celebrating. I spent Christmas day at one of the senior citizen homes, reading to a lady who didn't get any company."

He reached out unexpectedly and touched her hair. "I wouldn't have guessed you had so many soft spots. Sara. Isn't it?"

She nodded, thrilled by the faint caress. "Sara Dobbs."

He smiled tenderly. "I'll be in touch."

She smiled back, her eyes twinkling with emotion. "See you."

He drove off in a fancy red sports car like ones she'd seen on televised auto shows. She smiled as she considered his interest in her because of Grandad's favorite subject. First Harley, now the iron cowboy. She felt better than she had in years.

But she wondered if her ogre would still be interested if he found out how young she was. She'd just keep that to herself, she decided, like her past. There was no need for him to know anything about either subject yet. And by the time there was . . . well, maybe it wouldn't matter anymore.

On Thursday, when she got home from work, she sorted out Grandad's books, carefully pairing subject matter with time period, in case Jared Cameron wanted to borrow one. She knew her grandfather wouldn't have minded. He enjoyed teaching students about the amazing contradictions of the North African theater, where what many called a "gentleman's war" was fought. Rommel had actually called a truce during one bloody battle and sent his men to help move Allied wounded off the battlefield.

Patton had entered the campaign too late to face off against Rommel, but he had read Rommel's book about the strategy and tactics of World War I. The general was known for his own lightning strike sort of attack; he said that fewer soldiers were lost when battles were won quickly. Both soldiers led from the front, and both were respected by not only their own men, but by the enemy as well.

Her hands touched a book by a missionary who'd worked in Africa and stilled. This had been one of Grandad's favorite biographies, although it had nothing to do with World War II. The author of the book was a physician. He'd gone to Africa, sanctioned as a missionary, and remained there for many years treating natives. The book had inspired Grandad to missionary work, but he'd chosen to become a college educator instead. He'd regretted his decision later in life and had sold the idea wholesale to his daughter's husband.

Sara put the book aside, shoving it into a bookcase with undue savagery. If only he'd realized what the consequences of his fervor for mission work would be . . .

She stacked the books she was through sorting and got up. Morris was crying to be fed.

As she moved into the kitchen, she felt suddenly nauseous, and that pain in her stomach came back full force. She managed to get the sack of dry cat food and poured some of it into his bowl. Then she sat down and groaned. She was so sick she could barely move. It hurt to move, anyway.

She rested her forehead on her forearm, draped across the scarred little kitchen table where she and Grandad always had meals. She was sweating. It wasn't that hot in the house. She had a window air conditioner, and it was running full tilt.

These sick spells were getting closer together. Could she be having the same virus week after week? she wondered. Or could it be something else?

Her grandmother had suffered from gallbladder disease. She remembered, barely, the old lady being taken to the hospital when Sara was about four years old to have an operation. Doctors had removed it. She recalled that old Mrs. Franklin had complained of terrible pain in her stomach and feeling nauseous.

But gallbladder problems were in the upper right area of the abdomen. This felt like it was dead-center. Could she possibly have an ulcer?

It would pass, she told herself. She'd just sit very still and not move around and it would go away, like it always did. But it didn't go away. An hour later, it hurt to walk and nausea washed over her unexpectedly. She barely made it to the bathroom in time to lose her breakfast. The pain was horrible. She'd never felt anything like it. She felt feverish as well. Something was wrong. Something bad.

She crawled to the phone in the living room and

pulled it down on the floor with her. She pressed in 911.

When the dispatcher answered, she gave her symptoms and then her name and address. The lady told her to stay on the line while she sent the paramedics out.

Sara leaned back against the wall, so sick she couldn't bear the thought of being moved. The pain was in her side, her right side. It was so bad that even the lightest touch of her fingers caused her to jump.

Morris, sensing that something was wrong, came into the living room and rubbed against her, purring. She petted him, but she couldn't let him get into her lap.

Fortunately she hadn't locked up for the night. She'd managed to reach up and turn on the porch light. When the paramedics knocked, she shouted for them to come in.

One of them was a girl she'd gone to high school with, a brunette with short hair who'd been kind to her when other students hadn't been.

"Hi, Lucy," Sara managed as the woman bent over her with a stethoscope.

"Hi, Sara. Where does it hurt?"

Sara showed her. When Lucy pressed her fingers against it, Sara came up off the floor, groaning.

The three paramedics looked at each other.

Lucy put the thermometer into Sara's ear. "A hundred and two," she remarked. "Any nausea?"

"Yes," Sara groaned.

"Okay, we're taking you in to the hospital. What do you need us to do?"

"Get my purse on the sofa and make sure I've turned off everything and then lock the door with the key that's in this side of the dead bolt," she said weakly.

"Will do. Curt, can you check the appliances and turn off the lights?"

"Sure. What about the cat?"

"He can stay here, he's been fed and he has a litter box. I'll get my boss to run out and feed him tomorrow . . ." She sat back with a sigh. "My goodness, it stopped hurting," she said, smiling at Lucy. "I may not need to go to the hospital . . ."

"Get her loaded, stat!" Lucy said at once, and moved away to speak into the microphone on her shoulder so that Sara couldn't hear. She nodded as the reply came back. When she turned, Sara was on her way into the ambulance, arguing all the way. She wouldn't know until hours later that the cessation of pain had been a signal that her appendix had perforated. If she'd argued successfully to stay home, she'd have been dead by morning.

Four

It was all a blur to Sara. She was surprised that they'd prepped her for surgery and had her sign a consent form only minutes after she arrived at the hospital.

Dr. "Copper" Coltrain, the redheaded local surgeon,

was already masked and gowned when they wheeled her in.

"Hi, Dr. Coltrain," Sara said, her voice drowsy from the preop meds. "Are you going to carve me up?"

"Only your appendix, Sara," he replied with a chuckle. "You won't even miss it, I promise."

"But it feels fine now."

"I imagine so. That's a very bad sign. It means it's perforated."

"What's that?" she asked, while a capped, gowned and masked woman beside her put something in a syringe into the drip that led down to the needle in her arm.

"It's something to make you comfortable," came the reply. "Count backward from a hundred for me, will you?"

Sara smiled, sleepy. "Sure. One hundred, ninety-nine, ninety-eight, ninety . . ."

She came to in the recovery room, dazed and completely confused. She wanted to ask them what they'd done to her, but her lips wouldn't work.

A nurse came in and checked her. "Awake, are we?" she asked pleasantly. "Good!"

"Did Dr. Coltrain take out my appendix?"

"Yes, dear," the nurse replied.

Sara closed her eyes again and went back to sleep.

One of the great unsolved mysteries of small town life is how quickly word gets around if someone local is injured or killed. The process seems to consist largely of word of mouth. Someone who works at the hospital is related to someone who owns a small business, and phone traffic increases exponentially. Soon after the incident, it's an open secret.

Exactly how Jared Cameron found out that Sara's appendix had gone ballistic was never known. But he showed up about the time they'd moved Sara into a semiprivate room.

Tony Danzetta came with him and stood quietly outside the hospital room while Jared walked into it. The nurse who was making Sara comfortable and checking her vitals did a double take when she saw him and his companion.

"Don't mind Tony," Jared told her. "He goes everywhere with me."

Sara peered at him past the nurse. "Don't worry about it," she told the nurse in a still-drowsy tone. "He's not the only man who carries protection around with him."

The nurse burst out laughing. So did Jared.

Sara closed her eyes and drifted off again.

The second time she awoke, it was to find Jared lounging in the chair beside her bed. He was wearing working clothes. He looked really good in denim, she considered through a mixture of drugs and pain. He was very handsome. She didn't realize she'd said it out loud until he raised both eyebrows.

"Sorry," she apologized.

He smiled. "How do you feel?"

"I'm not sure how to put it into words." She looked past him at Tony, still standing patiently outside her room. "I seem to have lost my appendix. Do you suppose you could send Tony the Dancer out to look for it?"

"It's long gone by now. You'll improve. While you're improving, I'm taking you home with me."

She blinked. "That will cause gossip."

"It won't matter to your friends and what your enemies think doesn't matter to you. Or it shouldn't."

"Put that way," she agreed, "I guess you're right."

"You can't stay at your house alone, in this condition."

"What about Morris?"

"Tony the Dancer drove over to your house and fed him on his way here," he said carelessly. "He'll look after your cat until you're able to go home."

She was too groggy to wonder how Tony had gotten inside her house. The EMTs had locked it. She moved and grimaced. "I didn't realize that an appendix could kill you."

"It can if it perforates. Those stomach pains you were having were probably a symptom of chronic appendicitis," he said.

"I guess so. I never thought it might be dangerous. How long have you been here?"

"Since they took you in to surgery," he said surprisingly. "Tony and I went out to supper until you were in recovery, then we sat in the waiting room until they put you in a room."

Her eyelids felt heavy. "It was nice of you to come."

"We're each other's family, remember?" he asked, and he didn't smile. "I take responsibilities seriously."

"Thanks," she said weakly.

"Not necessary. Try to go back to sleep. The more rest you get, the faster you'll heal."

She stared at him a little drowsily. "Will you be here, when I wake up?"

"Yes," he said quietly.

She tried to smile, but she wasn't able to get her lips to move. She fell back into the comfortable softness of sleep.

It hurt to move. She tried to turn over, and it felt as if her stomach was going to come apart. She groaned.

The big man who went around with the ogre came and stood over her. He had large dark eyes, and heavy black eyebrows. His dark, wavy hair was in a ponytail. He had an olive complexion. He was frowning.

"Do you need something for pain?" he asked in a voice like rumbling thunder.

Her eyes managed to focus. He looked foreign. But he had that Georgia drawl. Maybe he was of Italian heritage and raised in the South.

He grinned, showing perfect white teeth. "I'm not Italian. I'm Cherokee."

She hadn't realized that she'd spoken her thoughts

aloud. The painkilling drugs seemed to be affecting her in odd ways. "You're Mr. Danzetta," she said. "I thought you were a hit man."

He laughed out loud. "I prevent hits," he replied. "I'm Tony. Nobody calls me Mr. Danzetta." The frown was back. "It hurts, huh?"

"It does," she managed weakly.

He touched the call button. A voice came over it. "May I help you?"

"This young lady could use something for pain," he replied.

"I'll be right there."

Minutes later, a nurse came into the room, smiling. "Dr. Coltrain left orders so that you could have something for pain."

"It feels like my body's been cut in half," Sara confessed.

"This will help you feel better," she said, adding something to the drip that was feeding her fluids. "It will be automatic now."

"Thanks," Sara said, grimacing. "I sure never thought losing a tiny little thing like an appendix would hurt so much."

"You were in bad shape when you came in," she replied. She glanced at Tony the Dancer curiously. "Are you a relative?"

"Who, me? No. I work for Mr. Cameron."

The nurse was confused. "Is he related to Miss Dobbs?"

Tony hesitated. "Sort of."

"No, he's not," Sara murmured, smiling. "But Mr. Cameron doesn't have any family left, and neither do I. So we said we'd take care of each other if one of us got sick."

"The boss said that?" Tony asked, his dark eyebrows arching.

The nurse frowned. "How can you be deaf with ears like that?" she wondered.

Tony glared at her. "I am not deaf."

"I should think not," she agreed, paying deliberate attention to his large ears.

"Listen, I may have big ears, but you've got a big mouth," he shot right back.

The pert little brunette gave him a gimlet stare. "The better to bite you with, my dear," she drawled. "You've been warned."

She wiggled her eyebrows at him before she turned back to Sara. "If you need me, just call. I'm on until midnight."

"Thanks," Sara told her.

She winked, gave the bodyguard a glance and waltzed out of the room.

Tony made a rough sound in his throat. "My ears are not big," he muttered.

Sara wouldn't have dared disagree.

He glowered. "People are supposed to be nice to you in hospitals."

"Only when you're sick," Sara told him, smiling. "Thanks, Tony," she said as the pain began to diminish, just a little.

"No problem."

"Where's Mr. Cameron?"

"He had a phone call to return," he said, and looked worried.

"Do you go everywhere with him?"

"Well, not everywhere," he replied. "He gets antsy if I follow him into the restroom."

"I never knew anybody who had a bodyguard," she told him. She moved drowsily. "In fact, I never knew a bodyguard."

"First time for everything," he said, and he smiled.

She smiled back. He'd looked frightening the first time she saw him, standing beside Jared's truck outside the bookstore. But now he was starting to resemble a big teddy bear. She closed her eyes and went to sleep, but not before she heard a soft, deep chuckle. She'd said it aloud.

Jared walked in with a scowl, pausing to stare at Sara, who was fast asleep. "Did they give her something for pain?" he asked Tony.

The big man nodded. He wasn't smiling now. He looked both intelligent and dangerous. "Is something going on?"

Jared looked toward the door, paused to push it shut and put his cell phone away. "Max thinks they may have tracked me here."

"That isn't good," Tony replied.

"We expected it," Jared reminded him. "We'll have to be extravigilant is all. I told the foreman to put a man with a rifle at the front gate and keep him there, even if he has to have catered meals." He cursed under his breath. "I hate hiding out," he said harshly. "If they'd let me do what I please, we could have handled this on our own, and more efficiently. They're going to protect me to death!"

"Not here," Tony said slowly. "You know they're doing the best they can. Meanwhile, this is the best place to be."

Jared let out a long breath. "It's the waiting."

Tony nodded. He glanced toward the bed. "What about her?" he asked. "She isn't going to be in the line of fire, is she?"

The other man stuck his hands in his pockets and looked stern. "She hasn't got anybody else."

"Yes, but she has no idea what's going on. She could become a target."

Jared glared at him. "Then you'll just have to call in a marker and get some backup, won't you?"

Tony sighed. "I gave up a hot tub and HD TV to come down here."

The glare got worse. "Don't blame me. I was willing to come alone. Your *boss* decided I needed baby-sitting," Jared said irritably.

"My boss was right," Tony replied. He shrugged. "I guess I can live without the hot tub for a few weeks."

Jared put a hand on his shoulder. "Sure you can. You need to reread Sun Tzu."

"I can quote it verbatim," Tony told him. "This isn't my first job."

Jared chuckled. "No. Of course it's not." He stared back at Sara. "We can't let them hurt her."

"We won't," Tony replied. "I promise."

Jared relaxed a little. But just a little.

Sara woke up and it was dark again. She'd slept for a long time. She looked around curiously. She was alone, but there was a cowboy hat occupying the seat beside her bed. It looked familiar.

The door opened, and Harley Fowler walked in, carrying a foam cup of coffee. "You're awake," he exclaimed, smiling.

"Hi, Harley," she replied, returning the smile. "Nice of you to come check up on me."

"I had tonight free."

"No date?" she asked with mock surprise as he moved his hat and sat down.

He chuckled. "Not tonight."

"No exciting missions, either?" she teased, recalling that he'd helped some of the local mercs shut down a drug dealer two years before.

"Interesting that you should mention that," he replied, his eyes twinkling. "We've had word that the drug cartel has reorganized again and been taken over by a new group. We don't know who they are. But there's some buzz that we may have trouble here before long."

"That's not encouraging," she said.

"I know." He sipped coffee. He looked somber. "Two DEA agents bought it on the border this week.

Execution-style. Cobb's fuming. My boss is calling in contacts for a confab." His boss was Cy Parks, one of the small town's retired professional soldiers.

Cobb was Alexander Cobb, a senior Houston DEA agent who lived in Jacobsville with his wife and sister.

"Does anybody know who the new people are?"

He shook his head. "We can't find out anything. We think somebody's gone undercover in the organization, but we can't verify it. It's unsettling to have drug dealers who'll pop a cap on cops. They killed a reporter, too, and a member of the Border Patrol."

She whistled softly. "They're arrogant."

He nodded. "Dangerous," he said. "There's something worse. They're kidnapping rich Americans for ransom, to increase their cash flow reserves. They got an heiress last week. Her people are scrambling to meet the deadline, without knowing for sure if they'll return her even so."

She moved restlessly on the pillow. She was sore, but the pain was better. "Aren't most kidnap victims killed in the first twenty-four hours?"

"I don't know, honestly," he said. "Cash Grier is working with the FBI, trying to get informants who might know something about the heiress."

"Our police chief?" she asked.

He grinned. "Like a lot of our local citizens, he's not quite what he seems."

"Oh."

He stretched. "Mr. Parks had me working on our tractor all day. I'm stiff. I guess I'm getting old."

She laughed. "No, you aren't, Harley."

He leaned forward with the cup in both hands. "I heard you had a close call," he said.

"I didn't know I had an appendix until yesterday," she said wistfully. "They brought me in by ambulance."

"What about Morris?"

"Mr. Danzetta fed him for me," she said complacently.

"Cameron's bodyguard?" He looked strange.

"What is it?" she asked curiously.

"One of our cowboys was driving past your house last night and saw lights on inside. He knew you were here, so he called the sheriff's department."

"And?"

"When they got there, the lights were off, the doors were all locked and there was nobody around."

She pursed her lips, wondering.

"Did you give the bodyguard a key?" he persisted.

She hesitated. "Well . . ."

Before she could speak, the door opened and Jared walked in. He stopped when he saw Harley and his eyes began to glitter.

Harley had great reflexes. He exercised them by getting out of the chair, wishing Sara well, promising to check on her later. He walked out with a nod to Cameron. He passed by Tony, who didn't say a word.

"You had company," Jared said quietly.

She wondered what he was thinking. His face gave little away. "Harley came to tell me about my house."

He frowned. "What about your house?"

"He said one of the Parks cowboys saw lights on inside and knew I wasn't there, so he called the sheriff," she began. "But when the deputy got there, all the lights were out and nobody was anywhere around."

He managed to look innocent. "How odd."

He looked too innocent. She frowned. "I didn't give Mr. Danzetta a key to my house, so how did he get in to feed Morris?"

He sat down in the chair beside the bed, looking thoughtful for a minute. "Tony has some, shall we say, unexpected skills."

"Like breaking and entering?" she probed with a grin.

"This is a conversation we shouldn't have right now," he replied with a quiet smile.

Her eyebrows lifted. "Is he wanted by the law?" she asked, keeping her voice low so that Tony wouldn't overhear her.

"Only in two countries," he said absently. "Or was it three?"

She looked shocked.

He scowled at her. "I'm kidding!"

She relaxed. "Okay," she said. "That's a relief."

Outside the door, a tall, dark-eyed man was chuckling silently.

"I talked to Dr. Coltrain," Jared said. "He told me if

you're still improving like this, you can be released Monday."

She grimaced. "I'll miss work." Her eyes widened. "Oh, gosh. Dee! I didn't even phone her . . . !"

"I did," Jared said lazily. "She's coming to see you tonight."

"Thanks," she told him.

"She already knew, of course," he added ruefully. "It's amazing how gossip gets around here."

"We're a very small town," she reminded him.

"You're a very large family," he contradicted. "I've never lived in a place where people knew so much about each other."

She smiled. "I know. I love it here. I can't imagine living anywhere else."

"Well, you'll be living with me for a few days," he replied, crossing his long legs. "My attorney's coming down Monday, so we'll be chaperoned. Less gossip."

"Does your attorney come to stay?"

"Only when I have legal matters to discuss," he said easily. "I've had the same attorney for two years."

She was picturing a tall lawyer like Blake Kemp. Jared must be very well-to-do if he could get a live-in attorney, she was thinking.

"Don't mention anything about Tony feeding your cat, okay?" he asked abruptly. "I don't want the police asking any embarrassing questions. I need Tony."

"Of course I won't," she agreed, but she couldn't

help wondering what all the secrecy was about.

"I can't stay long tonight," he said apologetically. "I'm trying to do business by phone, fax and modem, and it's damned hard."

Her eyes were curious. "Where do you live when you're not here?"

He smiled. "That's need-to-know. You don't."

"Well!" she exclaimed. "What a lot of cloak-and-dagger stuff!"

"You have no idea," he replied absently.

The door opened. Tony came in, flipping his phone shut. "Max needs to talk to you again. It's going to take a while."

"We'll go home." He got up, pausing to smile down at Sara. "Get better. I'll be back in the morning."

"Thanks," she said.

He shrugged. "We're family."

He went out with Tony and closed the door behind him.

Max was not happy to learn that Jared was keeping company with some sick girl in the little hick town.

"You need your head read," she muttered on the phone. "You've got enough problems without adding a penniless, clinging cowgirl to them."

"She's not a cowgirl," he replied. "She sells books."

"An egghead isn't much better," she scoffed. "They want you to come back out here and let them give you around-the-clock security."

"We'll never catch the perpetrators if we hide in a

fortress," he said. "And we've had this damned argument before!"

"Somebody's getting testy," she purred. "No pillow talk down there, I guess?"

"What do you want?" he interrupted.

She hesitated. "I wanted to tell you that they've tracked three men as far as San Antonio. We're not sure if they're connected to the other, or not, but they're the right nationality."

"What's their cover?"

"How should I know?" she muttered.

"I pay you to know everything," he countered.

"Oh, all right, I'll ask questions. Honestly, Jared, you're getting to be a grouch. What's this girl doing to you?"

"Nothing," he said tersely. "She's just a friend."

"You're spending a lot of time at the hospital."

"Neither of us has family," he said absently. "We decided we'd look after each other if we got sick."

The pause was heated. "You know I'd take care of you if you got sick! I'd have doctors and nurses all over the place."

Of course she would, he thought. She'd hire people to care for him, but she wouldn't do it herself. Max hated illness.

"I'm tired and I've got a lot of work to do."

"I'm flying down there Monday," she told him. "I'll bring some contracts for you to look over. Need anything from the big city?"

"Nothing at all. I'll talk to you later."

"Okay. Sleep well."

"Sure." He hung up. Max was possessive of him. He hadn't noticed it before, and he didn't like it. She was sleek, elegant, aggressive and intelligent. But she did nothing for him physically. He did have occasional liaisons, but never with Max. He hoped she wasn't going to come down to Texas and upset things. He knew that she wasn't going to like Sara. Not at all.

Monday morning, Sara was on the mend. Dee had come twice, on Friday night and Sunday afternoon, bearing baskets of flowers and magazines for Sara to read. She absolutely forbade her to come back to work until the end of the next week. That made Sara feel a little better. She knew Dee was shorthanded when she wasn't there.

Jared had been back to visit, staying for a few minutes at a time, with Tony always in the background. She wondered why he needed a full-time bodyguard. He changed the subject every time she asked.

Dr. Coltrain released her after lunch. She was wheeled out to the hospital entrance, where Jared was waiting in the big black pickup truck. He bent and lifted her like a sack of flour, putting her gently into the passenger seat and belting her in.

She didn't expect the sudden rush of breath that escaped her lips when he paused in the act of fastening the seat belt and looked straight into her eyes at point-blank range. She felt the world shift ten

84

degrees. His eyes narrowed and dropped to her blouse.

It didn't take an expert to realize that he saw her heartbeat shaking the fabric and knew that she was attracted to him.

"Well, well," he murmured in a deep, sultry tone. And he smiled.

Five

Jared's green eyes burned into Sara's, probing and testing. They dropped to her full mouth and lingered there until she caught her breath audibly. He only chuckled. It had a vaguely predatory sound.

He went around to his own side of the truck, climbed in, fastened his seat belt and started the engine. He was still smiling when he pulled out of the hospital parking lot.

Sara had liked the White Horse Ranch from her first close-up look at it, the first time she'd delivered Jared's books to him. She admired the sprawling white ranch house with its hanging baskets of flowers and the white wooden fences that surrounded a well-manicured pasture. Jared ran purebred Santa Gertrudis cattle here, not horses. Sara enjoyed watching the calves. Pastures were full of them in spring, just in time for the lush new grass to pop up. Or, at least, that would have been the case if the drought hadn't hit this part of Texas so hard.

"How do you have green grass in a drought?" she asked suddenly.

He smiled. "I sank wells and filled up tanks in every pasture," he replied, using the Texas term for small ponds.

"Not bad," she remarked. "Do those windmills pump it?" she added, nodding toward two of them— one near the barn and another far out on the horizon. He glanced at her amusedly. "Yes. It may be an old-fashioned idea, but it was good enough for the pioneers who settled this country."

"Your grandfather, was he born here?"

He shook his head. "One of his distant cousins inherited a piece of property and left it to him. He ranched for a while, until his health got bad." His face seemed to harden. "He took a hard fall from a bucking horse and hit his head on a fence. He was never quite right afterward. He put a manager in charge of the ranch and moved up to Houston with his wife. One summer day, he shot my grandmother with a double-barreled shotgun and then turned it on himself."

Her gasp was audible.

He noted her surprise. "My father brought him down here to be buried, although nobody knew how he died. None of the family ever came back here after that," he said. "I guess we all have something in the past that haunts us. I shouldn't have been so blunt about it," he added, when he realized that she was upset. "I forget that you grew up in a small town, sheltered from violence."

Obviously he considered her a lightweight, she mused. But it was too soon for some discussions. "It's all right."

He pulled up in front of the house, cut the engine and went around to pick Sara up in his strong arms and carry her up the three wide steps to the front porch. He grinned at her surprise.

"Coltrain's nurse said to keep you off your feet for another day," he mused, looking down into her wide, soft green eyes.

"So you're becoming public transportation?" she teased, and her smile made her whole face radiant.

It made her look beautiful. He was captivated by the feel of her soft, warm little body in his arms, pressed close to his chest. He loved that smile that reminded him of a warm fire in winter. He liked the surge of excitement that ran through his hard body at the proximity. His eyes narrowed and the smile faded as he held her attention.

"Listen, don't you get any odd ideas," she cautioned with breathless humor. "He didn't do that buttonhole surgery, he split me open at least six inches and sewed me back up with those stitches that you don't have to take out later. We wouldn't want my guts to spill out all over your nice clean floor, now, would we?"

The comment, so unexpected, caused him to burst out laughing.

"Good God!" he chuckled. He bent and brushed his hard mouth over her lips in a whisper of sensation that caused her entire body to clench. It was a rush of sensation so overwhelming that she felt her breath catch in her throat.

His eyebrows arched at her response. He pursed his lips and his green eyes twinkled. "What a reaction," he murmured deeply. "And I barely touched you." The twinkle faded. "Suppose we try that again . . . ?"

She started to give him ten good reasons why he shouldn't, but it was already too late.

His hard mouth crushed down onto her soft lips, parting them in a sensuous, insistent way that took her breath away. Her eyes closed helplessly. Her cold hands slid farther around his neck as his arm contracted and flattened her soft breasts against the wall of his chest. The kiss grew demanding.

"Open your mouth," he bit off against her bruised lips.

She tried to answer that audacious command, but it gave him the opening he was looking for, and he took it. His tongue moved deep into her mouth, accompanied by a groan that sounded agonized.

He felt her shiver in his arms. His mouth roughened for an instant until he realized that she was just out of the hospital, and her side hadn't healed. He lifted his head. His eyes were blazing. His face was set, solemn, his gaze intent on her flushed skin.

"Wh . . . why?" she faltered, all eyes.

An odd expression crept over his face. "When you smile, the emptiness goes away," he said in a rough whisper.

She didn't know how to answer that. But she didn't have to. The door opened suddenly, revealing a tall, very attractive brunette in a blue business suit with a short skirt that stopped halfway between her knees and her panty line.

The brunette raised an eyebrow at the sight of Jared with Sara in his arms, and she didn't smile. "Didn't you expect me, darling?" she asked Jared in a honey-smooth tone.

Jared was still collecting his senses. "Max, this is Sara Dobbs. Sara, Max Carlton, my attorney."

Sara had never seen an attorney who looked like that. The woman could have posed for a fashion magazine. She was sophisticated, beautiful and world-wise. Sara felt like a small child trying to play with adults.

"I have to get Sara to bed. Where's Tony?"

Max shrugged. "I haven't seen him. We have several contracts to go over."

"We'll get to them later," Jared said, with an edge to his tone.

"Suit yourself, it's only money. I like the house."

The lawyer had yet to say one word to Sara. Jared noticed, and his irritation was obvious.

"Sara, you said?" Max asked, smiling at the woman in his arms. "Is something wrong with your leg?"

"She just had an emergency appendectomy and there's nobody at her house to look after her while she heals," Jared said shortly, turning toward one of the downstairs guest bedrooms.

"I see. Well, I'm sure you'll feel better soon," she told Sara as Jared carried her down the hall.

Jared ignored her. He turned into a pretty blue-themed bedroom with its own private bathroom and eased Sara down on the quilted coverlet.

He leaned over her, his big hands on either side of her head, and looked straight into her eyes. "Max is my lawyer. That's all she's ever been."

"She likes you," Sara replied.

His green eyes narrowed. "She likes my money."

"She's pretty."

He bent and brushed his mouth softly over her lips, smiling as they parted for him now. "So are you," he whispered, standing up straight. "I have to sign some contracts for Max. I'll be back in a few minutes. TV control's on the bedside table," he indicated. "We have pay-per-view. Help yourself. I'll have Mrs. Lewis bring you something to eat in a little while."

"Mrs. Lewis? I thought she worked for the Hart brothers."

"She did, but she had to retire just recently from doing heavy housework. Her arthritis got steadily worse and she had to leave them. But her doctor found a new drug that works. She still can't do heavy work, but she cooks for me three days a week."

She studied him curiously. "What do you do the other four days?"

He grinned. "I eat Italian."

"We don't have an Italian restaurant," she began.

"Tony the Dancer can cook," he told her. "He makes the best lasagna I've ever eaten."

She laughed. "He doesn't look like a cook."

"He doesn't look like a lot of things. Amuse yourself until I get Max out of here. I'll be back soon."

"Okay."

He winked at her and closed the door on his way out.

"Are you out of your mind?" Max raged. "The girl's poor! She's just after your money!"

He slid his hands deep into his pockets and glared back at her. "And you discovered that after exchanging two sentences with her, did you?"

Her lips tautened. "You can't get involved with the locals, Jared. You know that, and you know why."

He cocked his head and stared at her intently. "Why are you here?" he asked abruptly. "I can sign contracts at your office in Oklahoma City if I have to. I can't think of a single good reason for you to be underfoot."

Her eyes avoided his. "You're vulnerable right now. You might get involved with someone you'd walk away from if things were normal."

"I pay you a king's ransom of a retainer to look out for my business interests," he said, emphasizing the business. "You start poking your nose into my private life and I'll replace you with a man. After," he added deliberately, "I send a letter of explanation to the Oklahoma Bar Association."

Her anger was gone at once. She pulled herself together. "You're right, I was out of line."

"What contracts are we discussing, then?"

She seemed oddly disoriented. One hand went to her temple and she frowned. "You know, I can't remember."

"Then why don't you go back to your office and think about it?" he suggested.

She sighed. "Okay. But it's still not good sense to trust people you don't know too far," she added.

He didn't reply.

She went into the living room and picked up her attaché case. She laughed self-consciously. "I really just wanted to see how you were," she confessed.

"I'm fine."

"Take care of yourself."

He didn't answer that statement, either. He just stared at her with dark, brooding eyes until she went toward the front door.

"You'll call, if you need anything?" she asked at the door.

"If I need legal advice," he emphasized, "I will."

She grimaced. The door closed firmly behind her.

Jared stared into space as he wondered how he'd missed that possessiveness in Max. Had it been there all along, or was it just starting? She knew he didn't want involvement. He'd said so. Why had she come? Had she been checking up on him and found out about Sara?

He turned toward his study, still deep in thought.

She did have a point, about Sara. He knew almost nothing about her.

Tony the Dancer came in with a bag of groceries. He paused at the open study door.

"I met a stretch limo on my way back," he told Jared. "Was it Max?"

He nodded.

"What was she doing here?" he asked.

"God knows," Jared replied curtly. "Warning me off Sara, I guess."

"I thought it would come to that," Tony mused. "Max likes to live high, and she doesn't make quite enough to suit her tastes."

"Obviously. Her office had better be paying for that limo," he added. "I'm not picking up the tab."

"You should tell Arthur," the other man advised, naming the elderly accountant who lived in and took care of the accounts.

"I will. You cooking?"

"Unless you want to try again," Tony said warily. "I'm still trying to scrape the scrambled eggs off that iron skillet."

"You didn't say I had to grease it first," he growled.

Tony just shook his head. "How's the kid?" he asked, nodding toward the hall.

"She's a grown woman," Jared countered. "She's fine."

Grown woman? Tony wondered if his employer really thought that innocent in his spare bed was fair game. She put on a good front with Jared, but Tony could see through the camouflage, and he knew things that his boss didn't. He wondered if he should mention what he knew to the other man, but the phone rang and Jared picked up the receiver. Tony thought it must be fate, and he went off into the kitchen to cook.

Sara fussed when Mrs. Lewis had to come all that way to serve her a bowl of soup and a salad.

"I can walk, honestly," she protested gently. "You don't have to wait on me."

Mrs. Lewis just grinned as she slid the tray onto Sara's lap. "It isn't any trouble, dear. Tony will pick this up. I have to get back home. My sister's coming over to visit." She chuckled. "Tony's making supper for you and the boss tonight. He walked in with enough Italian sausage and tomato sauce to float a battleship."

Now Sara remembered that Tony cooked Italian dishes for his boss. The big man didn't look like anybody's idea of a chef. She said as much to the older woman.

Mrs. Lewis raised an eyebrow. "Mr. Danzetta is in a class of his own as a cook. I can do basic meals, but he has a flair for improvising. He saved me a plate of spaghetti just after I came to work here. It was the best I ever tasted."

"I never thought of a bodyguard as being a cook," Sara commented.

The older woman glanced at the open door and moved a little closer. "He wears an automatic pistol under his jacket," she said softly. "I watched out the kitchen window while he was practicing with it. He stuck pennies in clothespins and strung the clothespins on an old wire that was used for a clothesline years ago. And in a heartbeat," she added, "he'd picked off the pennies without touching the clothespins."

Sara's eyes grew wide. "I'm going to make sure that I never tick him off," she murmured aloud.

"He's pretty handy with martial arts, too," Mrs. Lewis added. "He spars with Mr. Cameron."

She hesitated with the soup halfway to her mouth in a spoon. "Mr. Cameron does martial arts?"

Mrs. Lewis nodded. "Tony said he'd never met a man he couldn't throw until he started working here."

"And here I thought Mr. Cameron hired Tony because he didn't want to get his hands dirty."

"Tony isn't quite what he seems," the older woman said quietly. "And neither is his boss. They're both very secretive. And they know Cy Parks and Eb Scott."

That was interesting, because Cy and Eb were part of a group of professional soldiers who'd fought all over the world. Several of the old group lived either in Jacobs County or in Houston and San Antonio.

"Well, that sounds very mysterious, doesn't it?" Sara murmured as she sipped the hot liquid. "This is wonderful soup, Mrs. Lewis. I can't make potato soup, but I love to eat it."

The older woman beamed. "I'm glad you like it."

Sara paused, thinking. "Mr. Cameron was in a huddle with Chief Grier at the symphony concert," she recalled. "They looked very solemn."

"Gossip says that a new group is trying to establish a drug smuggling network through here again."

"That might explain the serious faces," Sara replied. "Our police chief has solved a lot of drug cases, and made a lot of enemies to go with them."

"Good for him," Mrs. Lewis responded. "I hope they lock them all up."

Sara grinned. "Me, too." She shifted and groaned, touching her stomach under the floppy blouse she was wearing with jeans. "How can a little thing like an appendix cause so much trouble?" she wondered.

"You're lucky you were able to get to a phone," the older woman said gently. "People have died of appendicitis."

Sara nodded. She looked around the pretty blue room. "Mr. Cameron and I agreed that we'd be each others' families when we got sick, but I never expected to take him up on the offer this soon."

"He's a surprising person, isn't he?" she asked. "He seems so cold and distant when you meet him. But he's not like that at all when you get to know him. You wouldn't believe what he did to Mr. Danzetta . . ."

"And you can stop right there while you still have work," Jared said from the doorway. He sounded stern, but his eyes were twinkling.

Mrs. Lewis made a face at him. "I was only humanizing you for Sara, so she wouldn't think you were really an ogre . . ." She stopped and clapped a hand over her mouth and blushed.

"It's all right," Sara assured her between mouthfuls of soup. "I did used to call him an ogre, but he improves on closer acquaintance." She grinned at Jared.

He pursed his lips and looked pointedly at her mouth. She almost dropped her spoon, and he laughed softly.

"Well, if you don't need me for anything else, I'm going home," Mrs. Lewis told him. "Mr. Danzetta's got stuff to make supper."

"I saw the sack full of tomatoes and tomato sauce," Jared replied. "He's planted tomatoes out behind the house in what used to be a kitchen garden. Tomatoes, oregano, chives, sage and about twenty other spices I never heard of."

"He doesn't look like a gardener," Sara commented.

Jared didn't answer her. She didn't need to know about Tony just yet.

"He planted poppies in the flower garden," Mrs. Lewis said with obvious concern.

"He likes flowers," Jared began.

"You don't understand," Mrs. Lewis persisted. "He didn't plant California poppies. He planted the other kind."

He frowned. "What's your point?"

"We're barely inside the city limits," she said, "but the fact is, we are inside them. When they begin to bloom, Chief Grier will send one of his officers out here to pull them up."

Jared didn't mention that he'd like to see anyone do that with Tony watching. "Why?"

"They're opium poppies," Mrs. Lewis emphasized.

He whistled. "I'll bet Tony didn't realize it."

"Better tell him," Mrs. Lewis replied. "Before he gets in trouble with the law."

He was going to say that it was way too late for that, but he didn't dare. "I'll talk to him," he said.

"I'll see you tomorrow, then. Get better, dear," Mrs. Lewis added with a smile for Sara.

"I heal fast," Sara replied, grinning. "Thanks."

Jared went out to make some phone calls and Sara finished her soup and dozed off. When she opened her eyes again, it was getting dark outside. She hadn't thought about nightclothes, but it was obvious now that she'd arrived with only her purse and the clothes she'd had on when they transported her to the hospital. She didn't have anything to sleep in.

There was a wonderful smell of spices drifting down the hall. Seconds later, Tony stuck his head in the door.

"You like spaghetti?" he asked.

"I love it," she replied, smiling.

He smiled back. "I'm just about to take up the pasta," he said. "It fell off the wall when I threw it there, so it's got about two minutes left before it's al dente."

"Al who?" she asked.

He glowered at her. "Al dente," he repeated. "Just right for the teeth. When you throw it at the wall and it sticks, it's just right to . . ."

"What the hell have you done to my kitchen wall?" came a roar from down the hall.

"I have to check that the pasta's ready!" Tony called to him.

Jared stomped down the hall, glaring at his bodyguard. "You've got streaks all over the damned paint!"

"They wipe off, boss," Tony assured him. "Honest."

"You couldn't just stick a strand of it in your mouth and chew it to see if it's ready?" Jared grumbled.

Tony's eyebrows arched. "Who bit you?" he asked.

Jared's face was like iron. He looked furious. "The bread's burning."

Tony rushed back down the hall without another word.

Jared glared at Sara. "Harley Fowler's in the living room. He stopped by to see about you."

"That's nice of him."

"Nice." His green eyes were glaring. "I don't have time to run a hospital complete with visiting hours," he muttered.

She flushed with embarrassment. She hadn't expected Harley to come looking for her.

Jared backstepped at her expression. She'd just had surgery and he was acting like a jealous boyfriend.

He caught himself and tried to relax. It didn't work. Harley was poaching on his preserves. "I'll send him in. Don't encourage him to stay long or drop in unexpectedly again without calling first."

"I won't," she began, but he was already halfway down the hall before she got the words out. She felt terrible. She was imposing on him. She should never have suggested that they take care of each other when they got sick. It was apparent that Jared already regretted agreeing to it.

Harley didn't look much better than Sara did. His lips were compressed and he was carrying his wide-brimmed Western straw hat.

"How're you doing?" he asked.

She sighed. "I'm feeling much better," she said.

"You don't look it. Why don't I phone Lisa and see if you can stay with her and Cy until you're back on your feet?" he suggested.

"I really don't need looking after," she replied. She felt uneasy. "Harley, do you think you could drive me to my house?" she added in a low voice.

He scowled. "You're not well enough to look after yourself, Sara. You won't even be able to lift a gallon of milk until that incision heals."

"I don't drink milk and I want to go home." She pulled herself off the bed, grimacing because it hurt. Jared had her pain capsules, but she'd be damned if she was going to ask him for them. It was clear that he didn't want her here.

She moved to the foot of the bed. She'd forgotten

that Jared had carried her down the hall. Walking it was going to be an ordeal, and she didn't dare ask Harley to carry her, although she knew he would if she asked.

Harley's arm shot out and caught her as she began to weave. "Here, you're not able to do this, Sara," he said firmly.

"What the hell are you doing?"

Jared walked right around Harley, picked Sara up and put her back in the bed. "Stay there," he said shortly.

She flushed again. "I will not! I just asked Harley to drive me home."

Jared felt his height decrease. "You're not able to stay by yourself yet."

"I am so," she retorted.

Jared glared at Harley as if the whole thing was his fault.

"You'll take her out of this house over my dead body," Jared told the younger man. He said it very softly, but it was a threat. Harley had seen eyes like that over the barrel of a gun. The hair on the back of his neck stood up.

"I'm in the way here," Sara interrupted, sitting up. She winced and held her incision with her fingertips. "I've got frozen TV dinners and I need to get back and take care of Morris, anyway!"

"I fed the cat today," Tony the Dancer said from the doorway. He was wearing a huge white apron and holding a slotted spoon. He frowned. "Something wrong here?" he queried when he tallied up the taut faces.

"She's trying to escape," Jared muttered.

"Hey, don't you listen to him," Tony said firmly, pointing the spoon at Jared. "It was only the one time I dropped baking soda in the sauce by accident. This sauce is perfect. You don't need to run away on account of my cooking."

"You cook?" Harley exclaimed, looking at the tall, muscular man with the olive complexion and wavy black hair in a ponytail. He looked as dangerous as Jared Cameron. And Harley had reason to know what dangerous men looked like.

Tony glared at him. "Yeah. I cook. What's it to you?"

Harley actually moved back a step. "Nothing at all!"

"Lots of men cook," Tony said belligerently. He glanced back at Sara and frowned. She was near tears and she wouldn't look at Jared. Tony's threatening expression melted into concern. He moved to the side of the bed. "I made you a nice apple strudel for dessert," he coaxed, "with freshly whipped cream."

She bit her lower lip. "You're so nice, Tony," she said, trying to sound normal even as her lower lip quivered.

"Here, hold this." Tony put the spoon in Jared's hand and sat down beside Sara, tugging her gently against him so that he wouldn't hurt her. A hand the size of a ham rested against her back, covering almost half of it comfortingly as he drew her head to his broad shoulder. "Now, now, it's all right," he said softly.

She bawled. Jared and Harley glared daggers at the big man, but neither of them said a word.

Harley shifted on his feet. "Sara, I've got to get back home. You call me if you need anything, okay?" he added with a speaking glance at Jared.

"I will," Sara said in a thin, sad voice. "Thanks."

"No problem. See you."

He hated leaving her, but the whole situation was getting out of hand. That big fellow who cooked wasn't going to let Jared Cameron hurt Sara in any way. Harley knew she'd be safe, or he wouldn't have budged.

Jared walked out of the room behind him, totally disgusted, still carrying the spoon.

Six

Tony tugged a tissue from the box on the bedside table and dabbed it against Sara's wet eyes.

"Now you stop that," he said, smiling gently. "The boss has a nasty temper and he doesn't always choose his words before he opens his mouth. But he never would have asked you to come here if he hadn't wanted to."

She looked up at him from swollen red eyes. "He was awful to Harley."

Tony grimaced. "There's stuff going on that you

don't know about," he said after a minute. "I can't tell you what it is. But it doesn't help his temper."

She blew her nose. "I'm sorry."

"What for? Everybody cries," he replied. "I bawled like a kid when my sister died."

Her green eyes met his black ones. "Was it very long ago?"

"Ten years," he said. "Our mother was still alive then. We lost our dad when we were just little kids."

"I lost my grandad a little while ago," she replied. "I still miss him. He taught history at our local college."

"I like history," he said. He would have liked to tell her that he'd minored in it during his college years, but it wasn't the time for heart-to-heart talks. The boss was already gunning for him because he'd opened the door and let Harley inside.

"How long have you worked for Jared?" she asked.

"Seems like forever, sometimes," he chuckled. "On and off, for about six years, I suppose," he said.

"You know, he really doesn't look like the sort of man who'd need a bodyguard," she ventured.

"He doesn't, does he?" he agreed. "You feel better now?"

She smiled at him with her eyes still red and swollen. "I'm better. Thanks, Tony."

He stood up, and he was smiling now, too. "You're a lot like her. My sister, I mean. She had a big heart. She loved people. She was always giving." His dark eyes grew haunted, especially when he looked at

Sara. "Don't you let him push you into anything," he said out of the blue.

She was shocked, and showed it. "What do you mean?"

His black eyes narrowed. "You know what I mean. He's been around the world. You're just a sprout."

"Yes, but I can take care of myself," she assured him. "Nobody will make me do something I don't want to do."

"That's just what my sister said," he told her, and he looked down at his apron. "I'd better get back in there and rescue my sauce. You need anything?"

She shook her head. "But, thanks."

He grinned. "Goes with the job."

If she could have walked, she'd have gone home. She was hurt by Jared's sarcasm and she felt unwelcome. It was going to be an ordeal to get through the next couple of days. She wished she'd never become friendly with him. One thing was for sure. If she ever got sick or hurt again, she wouldn't turn to him for help.

He walked in a short time later with a plate of spaghetti and homemade garlic bread. He pulled a rolling table to the bed and put the meal, plus a tall glass of milk, on it.

She was rigid with wounded pride. "Thank you," she said stiffly, and in a subdued tone that betrayed, even more than her posture, how hurt she was.

He stood still, his hands in his pockets, and stared

at her. "He's a good cook," he said, just to break the silence.

She put the napkin on her lap and sat sideways on the bed so that she could eat comfortably. It put him at an angle so that she didn't have to look right at him.

"All right, I was out of line," he muttered. "But it's courteous to ask me before you invite people here to see you."

"I didn't invite Harley to come," she said, eating spaghetti in tiny little bites.

He frowned. "You didn't?"

She ate another bite of Tony's delicious concoction, and never tasted a thing.

"People who live in small towns think of everyone as family. It would never occur to Harley that he wasn't welcome to visit a sick friend, no matter who she was staying with."

His eyes kindled. "It's still good manners to ask first."

"Yes," she had to agree. "It is. I'm sure he wishes he had. I know I do."

That was right on target. He felt smaller than ever. She could have died. He'd agreed to take her home and nurse her, and now he was laying down rules and regulations as fast as he could. He didn't like Harley Fowler in his home, in Sara's temporary bedroom. It made him angry. He couldn't tell her that, of course.

He noticed suddenly that she was wearing the same clothes she'd worn to the hospital before her surgery.

"Don't you have a gown, or pajamas?" he asked abruptly.

"There really wasn't time to pack a bag when the ambulance got to my house," she reminded him.

"Point taken."

"If Tony could go by my house and get me some night things," she began.

"No." It came out belligerently. He shouldn't have said that. But he didn't like the idea of Tony, who already treated her like family, poking through her underthings.

"I'll go," he said. "Where's your house key?"

"It's in the zippered compartment in my purse." She indicated it, hanging over the closet doorknob. "Can you make sure Morris has enough water while you're there?" she added, hating even to have to ask. "Tony fed him already, he said, but Morris drinks a lot of water."

He retrieved the key. "I'll take care of him."

"Thanks," she said without meeting his eyes.

He gave her one last look and left her. He'd made a stupid mistake. He hoped he'd have time to make it up to her.

Tony was just clearing away supper when Jared stopped in the kitchen doorway. "I'm going over to Sara's house to get her a few things to wear."

Tony's eyebrows arched. "You know where she lives?"

He cursed mentally. Of course he didn't know where she lived; he'd never been to her house.

"And you can't go alone," the big man added solemnly. "They'd love to catch you out alone at night. They have all the equipment we've got, and more." He took off the apron and tossed it aside. "I'm going with you."

"That will leave Sara here alone," Jared argued.

Tony pointed a device down the hall and locks slid into place audibly. "She wouldn't be any safer in Fort Knox with the alarm systems activated," Tony told his boss. "Besides, I've got Clayton out there with night vision and a Glock."

He relaxed a little. "Okay. Let's go."

Tony paused by the closet on the way out and retrieved his .45 in its shoulder holster. He took just seconds to get it in place before he opened the front door and shepherded his boss out to the truck parked in the circular driveway.

Before they got into it, Tony waved his hand and a tall, shadowy figure approached the car, going over it with electronic devices.

"All clear," the newcomer said.

"Nobody gets in or out while we're gone," Tony told him.

"Yes, sir."

Tony climbed in behind the wheel, letting Jared ride shotgun. The shadowy figure moved back into the darkness beside the house and settled in.

While Jared was gone, the phone started ringing off the hook. Sara waited for Tony to answer it, but he didn't. There didn't seem to be an answering machine, either. She didn't know what to do. The stupid instrument wouldn't stop. Finally, in desperation, she picked up the receiver by her bed.

"Cameron residence," she said, trying to sound like a secretary.

"Where's Jared?" came a biting reply.

Sara didn't have to ask who it was. That strident tone was unforgettable. "I don't know," she said. "Sorry," she added quickly.

There was a pause. "It's the little house guest, isn't it?" the horrible woman purred. "Well, don't get too comfortable. Jared wouldn't give you the time of day if you hadn't appealed to his senses, but it won't last. He has women like some men have cars, and he doesn't want anything permanent. He'll dump you the first time you sleep with him."

"I do not sleep with men!" Sara retorted harshly.

"You don't?" She laughed. "That's what his last lover said, too. She gave in just like all the rest. And he dumped her just as fast."

"What do you want?" Sara asked, trying to be polite when she felt like screaming at the woman.

"What we all want, dear," the other woman laughed. "To have Jared for keeps. But that won't happen. If he wasn't so financially secure, he might be less attractive," she added.

"I know very little about Mr. Cameron," Sara said stiffly. "And I don't think you should talk about him that way. You're supposed to be his lawyer."

"His lawyer, his lover, it's all the same," came the bored reply. "Tell him I called."

She hung up.

Sara felt sick at her stomach. Surely the horrible woman wasn't right? Jared didn't seem like a heartless seducer. But what did she really know about him? Next to nothing. Could he be a ladykiller? Sara felt insecure. She was still very young. She hadn't dated very much and she'd never had to extricate herself from a dangerously intimate situation. She knew instinctively that Jared was experienced. She'd given in to his hard kisses at once. What if he really put on the pressure? Could she save herself in time?

The thought worried her.

She was still gnawing on it when Jared opened the door and came into her bedroom with a large laundry hamper.

Her eyebrows arched. "You brought my dirty clothes back with you?" she exclaimed, aghast.

He glowered at her. "Tony's got your clothes. I brought your cat."

Her heart skipped. He had to be kidding! She sat up on the side of the bed and looked down into the basket. There was old Morris, curled up asleep and purring for all he was worth, on one of her old hand-crocheted afghans.

She looked up at Jared curiously.

"He didn't touch his supper last night. He wouldn't eat today, either. Tony thinks he's worried about you.

So we brought him home with us." Gently he lifted the battle-scarred old marmalade tomcat out of the basket and placed him on the bed with Sara.

Morris opened one green eye, butted his head against Sara affectionately, and went right back to sleep.

"Tony's bringing the litter box. We can put it in your bathroom," Jared said disgustedly.

She cuddled Morris while he was in the mood. "He didn't try to bite you . . . ? Oh!"

He displayed a hand liberally covered with colorful plastic bandages.

"I'm really sorry," she began.

"I had an old hunting dog I was fond of," he said gruffly. "He died last month at the age of fourteen years." He shrugged. "They're like family."

She managed a tiny smile. "Yes."

He heard Tony coming down the hall. "I hope we got the right things."

Tony came in grinning and put down a suitcase on the chest at the foot of Sara's bed. "Here's your stuff. I'll bring the litter box when I come back. He's nice, your cat."

"Well, of course you'd think he was nice," Jared muttered. "He didn't sink his fangs into you!"

"He's got good taste," Tony defended himself.

"Good taste the devil, he knows that you've eaten cats!" Jared shot back. "He was probably afraid you'd serve him up for lunch if he bit you!"

Tony, noting Sara's expression, scowled. "It was

only one cat," he pointed out. "And we were all starving. It was a very old and very tough cat. Nobody liked it," he added, trying to hit the right note.

Sara was all eyes. "Where were you?" she asked, aghast.

"Somewhere in Malaysia," Tony said easily. "Mostly we ate snakes, but sometimes you got no choice, especially when the snakes can outrun you." He noted Sara's expression and stopped while he was ahead. "I'll just go get that litter box."

"You'd never be able to eat a snake he cooked," Jared muttered when Tony was in the hall. "He can't make anything if it doesn't go well with tomato sauce."

"I heard that!" Tony called back. "And snakes go great with tomato sauce!"

Sara smiled despite the rough time Jared had given her. He and Tony were a great act together. But she sensed undercurrents. And she thought both men were wearing masks, figuratively speaking. She wondered what they hid.

She finished her dinner and Jared still hadn't said another word.

"This was very nice," she said when she finished her last sip of milk and was pushing the rolling cart away from the bed. "Thanks." She eased back onto the bed, grimacing as the stitches pulled, and drew old Morris close to her. "He doesn't move much these days," she said as she stroked the purring old tomcat.

"I've never been sure how old he is. I don't think I want to know." She looked up at Jared. "I would have told you that he doesn't like being picked up, if I'd known you planned to bring him over here."

"Well, the minute Tony picked him up he started purring."

She hid a smile. "I'll bet animals follow Tony around."

He thought of a few women he and Tony had come across in their travels. "It isn't just animals," he said thoughtfully.

She stroked Morris again. "Your lawyer called."

He hesitated. "Max?"

She nodded.

"What did she want?"

She was weighing honesty against peace on earth. Peace on earth won. "She just wanted to tell you something. She said she'd call back."

He frowned. "Was that all she said?" he asked with visible suspicion. "No comments about your presence here?"

The blush gave her away.

"I thought so," he said. "She's good at what she does, but she bores easily and she likes new experiences. She can't resist setting her cap at every presentable male client who comes along. She's already gone through three husbands and several lovers."

Including you? she wondered, but she didn't dare say it out loud.

He watched her stroking the cat and it reminded

him, for some reason, of his grandmother. "My father's mother loved cats," he recalled. "She had six at one time. Then they began to get old and pass on. The last one she had was a yellow tabby, sort of like Morris. When she died, he stopped eating. We tried everything. Nothing worked. He settled down in the sun without moving and died three days later."

"And they say animals don't feel emotion," she murmured absently.

"Everything feels. Even plants."

She looked up, grinning. "Did you see that show where they put plants in little greenhouses . . ."

". . . They yelled and praised one group, ignored another group and played classical and rock music to two other groups," he continued, his green eyes twinkling.

"And the plants that grew biggest were the ones bombarded with hard rock."

He chuckled. "If I thought that would work on hay, I'd have loudspeakers set up in the fields." He shook his head. "First we had drought for a year in Oklahoma, now we're having floods. The weather is no friend to the rancher this year, either."

"Our dry fields could sure use some of your floods," she agreed.

The conversation ended. He was tired and half out of humor. She was getting over surgery.

"You need your rest," he said.

"Thanks," she called after him. "For bringing Morris."

"What's a little blood between friends?" he mused, holding up his scratched hand. "Sleep well."

"You, too."

But she didn't sleep well. She had violent dreams, just as she had as a child. There was something about this house, this atmosphere, that reminded her of all she'd lost. Guns shooting. Men yelling. Fires burning. The plane almost crashing. And then her mother's fury at Grandad, her accusations, her sudden bizarre behavior. The anger and rage in her mother never abated. Sara was left with nobody except Grandad to look after her. Her mother had destroyed herself, in the end. It had started out as a grand adventure with a noble purpose. It ended in bloodshed and death.

Sara pulled Morris closer to her in the big bed, wiping angrily at the tears. She hated going to sleep. She wondered if there would ever be a night when she'd sleep until morning and there would be no more bad dreams.

She touched her head where the faint indentation marked the most tragic part of her young life. It was under her thick blond hair, and it didn't show. But Sara felt it there. It was a constant reminder of how brief life was, and how dangerous. She thought about it when she looked at Tony Danzetta, but she couldn't understand why.

Finally, just before dawn she drifted off again. When she woke, late in the morning, it was to the realization that she was still wearing her jeans and the blouse. She'd been too preoccupied even to change into a nightgown.

She stayed with Jared for two more days. He seemed to be avoiding her. He didn't have breakfast, lunch or dinner at the table. He was always in his study or out with the cowboys on the ranch. Tony assured her that it was his normal routine, but something in the way Tony said it made her uneasy.

The fourth day after her surgery, she packed up Morris and her suitcase and asked Jared to let Tony take her home. She wasn't completely over the surgery, but she was getting around very well. There was some residual soreness, but she was already feeling better.

Jared didn't hesitate when she asked to go. It wounded her that he could let her walk away without a qualm. But, then, he was a financially secure man, from all appearances, and she was a poor woman. They'd agreed only to be each other's support in times of need, not to make the care permanent.

Sara and Morris settled back into their routine, and she went back to work.

"At least you look a little better," Dee commented, noting the dark circles under Sara's eyes. "I'll bet you didn't sleep a lot at Mr. Cameron's place."

"It was sort of awkward," she admitted. "But I saw

a lot more of Tony than I did of Mr. Cameron," she added.

"Tony?"

"The big guy."

"Oh," Dee recalled. "The hit man."

Sara chuckled. "He improves on closer acquaintance," she told her boss. "And Morris let Tony pick him up. He bit Mr. Cameron. Several times." It felt good, remembering that.

"I suppose Morris is a pretty good judge of character, then," Dee said with a grin.

"Now, now," Sara chided. "Mr. Cameron took good care of me while I was getting back on my feet."

Dee grimaced. "I could have taken you home with me," she began guiltily.

"Dee, you have four kids and your mother lives with you and your husband," Sara replied gently. "You couldn't possibly take care of one more person. But thank you for offering. I'm just grateful that I still have a job."

"As if I'd fire you for being sick," the older woman scoffed. "Now don't you do any heavy lifting. I'll do that. You just sit there at the counter and ring up purchases."

"I can do that, at least," Sara replied cheerfully.

It was just before closing time when Harley Fowler turned up. Dee had gone to the bank with the day's receipts while Sara waited for her to come back and lock up.

"Hi, Harley," Sara greeted.

He smiled. "You look lots better," he said. He grimaced. "I know I got you in trouble with Cameron by just walking in to see you. I'm really sorry."

She was stunned. "How did you find out about that?"

"Mrs. Lewis is kin to one of our cowboys. She heard Tony talking about it. I never thought Mr. Cameron would mind. I guess I should have asked first."

"He's an outsider, Harley," she said gently. "He doesn't know how people behave in small towns. Nobody else would have had a problem."

"I sort of wondered . . ." he began, and then stopped.

"Wondered?" she prompted.

"If Mr. Cameron might be jealous," he said.

She laughed. "Oh, that would be the day," she chuckled. "A big time rancher jealous of a piddly little clerk in a bookstore. He's got this gorgeous attorney, named Max," she added, trying to sound lighthearted. "She's educated and beautiful and crazy about him."

Harley sighed. "It must be nice to have a little money. I wouldn't know." He leaned on the counter with his forearms. "The Parks are having a barbecue at the ranch Saturday. Lisa said you might want to sketch the pups one more time before they're old enough to adopt. She says they're growing like weeds."

"A barbecue?" she echoed, smiling. "I love barbecue."

"I know," he returned, grinning. "Suppose I come and pick you up about eleven Saturday morning? I know you're still sore and all. I can drive you home whenever you need to go."

"I'd love to go, Harley," she said with genuine affection.

He smiled. She wasn't beautiful, but he liked being with her. "That's a date, then."

"Will there be dancing?" she asked.

"Oh, yes. They hired a Mariachi band to play. I understand there's going to be a major competition between the Caldwells and Cash Grier and his wife. A tango."

"Wow," Sara breathed. "Matt and Leslie were our champions hands down until Cash Grier got out on the dance floor with Christabel Gaines—I mean, Christabel Dunn, but that was before she married Judd. Can Tippy Grier do a tango?"

"Apparently. It's going to be a night to remember." He hesitated. "Your adopted family's invited, too."

"Mr. Cameron?" she asked warily.

"Yes, and the hit man, too."

"Tony is not a hit man," she said, laughing when she realized that it was her own description of him that was making the rounds in town. "I shouldn't have said that."

"He does sort of remind me of a hit man," he replied dryly. "He's big and slow-looking, though. He can't be that good a bodyguard."

Sara had doubts about how slow-moving Tony was.

She had the distinct impression that he was quick as lightning and sly like a fox, hiding his light under a barrel. But she didn't say so.

"Saturday at eleven," he repeated.

"Yes." She grinned at him as he waved and went out the door.

Sara pictured the band and Jared Cameron. She wondered if he'd ask her to dance. She wondered if he could dance. It was thrilling to consider.

Harley came for her exactly at eleven. She was wearing a full skirt with a simple white cotton peasant blouse and silver jewelry. She looked like a pixie.

He was in jeans and a clean plaid cotton shirt, Western cut, with polished black boots and a cowboy hat to match.

"You look nice, Sara," he told her. "Are you feeling okay?"

She nodded. "The stitches catch a little when I walk too fast, but I feel fine."

"Can you climb up by yourself?" he added when they reached his pickup truck. It had a running board, but it was higher than a car.

"Sure, I can," she said. She held on to the inside handle over the door facing, put one foot on the running board and pulled herself up and into the passenger seat. It hurt a little, but she didn't let that show. "Piece of cake," she told him, smiling while she fastened her seat belt.

He grinned back. "Then we're off!"

• • •

Cy Parks's ranch was huge, even by Texas standards. The yard was full of tent pavilions complete with oil-cloth-covered long tables and benches for people to sit on. The cowboys had barbecued a steer and their wives had prepared huge tubs of baked beans and coleslaw, and there were baking sheets full of home-made rolls and fresh butter. For dessert, there was everything from cakes to pies to soft-serve ice cream. Cy had really pulled out the stops. Across the fences, his Santa Gertrudis cattle grazed peacefully and stared at the crowds of people who'd come to enjoy the food.

All the powerful people in the county had shown up for Parks's legendary barbecue. Even the children were invited. It resembled, more than anything, a family reunion.

"Is that the Coltrains' little boy, Joshua?" Sara exclaimed, indicating a blond-headed little boy in jeans and cotton shirt and boots running from another small boy with dark hair and eyes.

"Yes, and that's J.D. and Fay Langley's little boy, Jon, chasing him."

"They've grown so fast!" she exclaimed.

"They have," he added, smiling at their antics. "Children must be a lot of fun. Their parents seem to dote on them."

"I imagine they do."

She was staring after the little boys when she spotted a familiar face. Jared Cameron was standing by one of the long tables talking to Cy Parks. With him were Tony the Dancer . . . and the female attorney, Max, standing with Jared's arm around her.

Sara felt as if she'd just walked into a nightmare.

<u>Seven</u>

At the same time Sara spotted him, Jared glanced her way and saw her with Harley Fowler. His green eyes, even at the distance, were blazing.

She averted her eyes and kept walking with Harley to where Lisa was sitting with Gil on her lap. She didn't dare look the way she felt. Jared Cameron had every right to hang out with his gorgeous attorney. It shouldn't have made Sara feel betrayed. But it did. The realization shocked her.

Lisa smiled as they joined her. "Have a seat. I could have left Gil in his playpen, but I don't really like being away from him, even for a few minutes."

"I wouldn't, either," Sara said. "He's a little doll."

Gil smiled at Sara shyly and said, "Pretty."

Sara and Lisa burst out laughing.

"Horsey, Mama, horsey!" Gil demanded, bouncing.

Lisa put him on one knee and bounced him while he laughed happily.

"He's going to be a ladies' man when he grows up," Harley drawled. "He's starting early!"

Lisa laughed. "You may be right. He likes Sara."

"Everybody likes Sara," Harley said smoothly, winking at her.

"Not everybody," Sara murmured as Jared Cameron walked toward them with Max curled close in his arm. He was smiling at Max, but his green eyes shot daggers at Harley and Sara when he came closer.

"Should you be up so soon after major surgery?" Jared demanded, glaring at Sara.

"Major surgery?" Sara gasped. "I had my appendix out! The incision was barely four inches long!"

Jared's eyes narrowed. "It ruptured," he pointed out.

"Why does he get to make comments on your surgery?" Lisa asked innocently.

"Because I took her home with me and Tony and I nursed her back to health," Jared said curtly. "We have a vested interest in her recovery."

"Like it put you out! Tony did all the work!" Sara retorted.

Jared held up his hand with all the plastic bandages on it.

"You didn't try to pick up Morris, did you?" Lisa asked the newcomer.

Jared looked around him, exasperated. "Am I the only person in this town who didn't know that he bites?"

"Looks like it," Harley chuckled.

"I hate cats," Max muttered. "They're scary, and they have fangs, like snakes."

Sara wished the other woman had been around when Morris was staying at Jared's house. She'd have loved watching him stalk the slick lawyer. He loved to attack people who were afraid of cats.

"Hi, Sara," Tony said, thickening his drawl for the group. He was wearing his suit and his sunglasses, and he looked really big. "You doing okay?"

Sara had gotten used to him being as articulate as Jared in the privacy of the Cameron ranch. Only now did she realize what a compliment he'd paid her by not putting on what was obviously an act for the masses.

"I'm much better, Tony, thanks," she replied, and gave him a genuine smile.

Max was looking more uncomfortable by the minute. "We aren't going to eat outside, are we?" she asked uneasily. "I mean, there are flies!"

"They only land on bad people," Sara promised.

Seconds later, two huge black flies came to rest on Max's arm.

She screamed, hitting at them. "Get them off!" she exclaimed.

Tony glanced at Sara and grinned. "Sound familiar?" he teased.

She burst out laughing, remembering her own horror at the yellow hornet that had landed on her shoulder at Jared's house.

But Max thought Sara was laughing at her and, without a pause, she swung her hand and slapped Sara in the face.

There was a sudden silence around them. Cy Parks, who'd been directing the cowboys cooking the beef, strode up to the small group with blood in his eye.

"Are you all right, Sara?" he asked in a menacing tone.

"I'm . . . fine," Sara replied. She had a huge red mark on one cheek.

Cy turned to Max. "I've never asked a guest to leave my home until now. I want you off my property."

Max fumed. "She laughed at me! I was covered up in flies and she thought it was funny!"

"She was laughing because the same thing happened to her at our place with a yellow hornet," Tony said, and he looked menacing as well. "I reminded her of it."

Max flushed. "Oh."

Jared hadn't said a word until then. But his eyes spoke volumes. "You can apologize to Sara before I take you back to the ranch," he told Max, and he wasn't smiling.

Max backed down at once. "I'm very sorry," she told the younger woman. "I hope I didn't hurt you," she added in a condescending tone.

Cash Grier joined the small group. He wasn't smiling, either. "If you'd like to press charges," he told Sara while he glared down at Max, "I'll be delighted to arrest her for you."

"Arrest me!" Max exclaimed.

"For assault," he replied coldly. "In Jacobsville, you don't strike another person physically unless you've been attacked physically. It's against the law."

"Yeah, you'd think a lawyer would know that,

wouldn't you?" Tony put in his two cents' worth.

Max seemed to be suddenly aware of her whereabouts and her vulnerability in this small town. She laughed nervously. "Surely that won't be necessary . . . ?"

Cash looked at Sara. "Sara?" he questioned softly.

Sara took a deep breath and gave Max her best glare. "I won't have you arrested," she said quietly. "But if you ever touch me again, I'll show you how much I learned in Chief Grier's self-defense course last fall."

"It won't happen again," Jared replied. He took Max firmly by the arm. "Thanks for inviting us," he told Cy, "but we have to go."

Tony grimaced. "Yeah. Sorry," he added, smiling at Sara. "That barbecue sure smelled good."

"Can't you stay?" Sara asked Tony gently.

He lit up like a Christmas tree at her tone.

Jared muttered something under his breath and Max protested as his hand tightened bruisingly on her arm.

Tony glanced at his boss and sighed. "No. I got to go, too. See you, Sara."

She smiled. "See you."

The three walked away with stiff backs. Sara could have kicked Max. She'd ruined everything.

"Thanks, Chief Grier," Sara told the town's police chief.

He shrugged. "You were my star pupil," he replied. He grinned. "I wish you'd pressed charges, though. I would have enjoyed locking her up."

"Locking who up?" Tippy Grier asked curiously, joining her husband. The "Georgia Firefly" as she'd been known in modeling circles was still gorgeous, with long reddish-gold hair and green eyes. She smiled at Sara, and then frowned when she saw the red marks on her cheek. "What in the world happened?" she exclaimed.

"Jared Cameron's lawyer hit her," Harley said angrily.

"A man hit you?" Tippy gasped.

"A woman," Sara corrected. "It was because of the flies."

Tippy stared at her, wide-eyed. "Flies. Right."

"No," Sara laughed. "I mean, she thought I was laughing at her because she attracted flies."

"Good riddance, I say," Harley muttered, watching Jared's Jaguar peel out and roar away. "The poor flies will probably drop dead now."

Sara was disappointed, because she'd hoped that she might have a chance to dance with Jared. But she hated herself for the thought. He'd been horrible to her about Harley, and now he'd sided with Max. But Tony had defended her. Sweet Tony.

"Who was the big fella with Jared?" Cash asked curiously.

"Tony the Dancer," Cy answered before Sara could. Everybody looked at him.

He realized at once what a slip he'd made. "I heard Jared call him that," he said at once.

They still looked at him. He'd used Jared's first

name, something he never did with strangers.

He cursed. "Just pretend I didn't say a word, and let's go and eat barbecue," he muttered. He bent to Lisa, smiling, and picked his little son up in his arms.

"Daddy!" Gil enthused, hugging his father around the neck.

The burned arm was still a little weak, but it didn't show. The look on his face as he held the little boy was indescribable.

"Gil's growing," Tippy said, smiling at the child.

"So is our Tris," Cash replied. "She's two now. Rory's twelve. He's crazy about his niece." Rory was Tippy's younger brother.

"Speaking of Tris," Tippy grinned, looking past her husband's shoulder.

Rory had little Tris up in his arms and was carrying her around, laughing. She looked just like her mother, with red hair and green eyes, and she was wearing a pretty little green-patterned cotton dress with white shoes. She was holding on to Rory for all she was worth, talking to him.

Rory, taller now, had dark hair and green eyes, and he obviously doted on the little girl.

"She can walk, you know," Cash told the boy with a smile.

"She likes it when I carry her, though," Rory replied, grinning. "Isn't she just the neatest thing in the world?" he added, kissing the little girl's hair.

"You're spoiling her," Tippy laughed.

Rory shook his head. "No, I'm not. I just carried her

away from the ice cream. She talked Randy into giving her a bowl of it, but I made him take it back."

"Wanted ice cream, Rory," Tris pouted. "Bad Rory."

He only chuckled.

Tippy held out her arms for Tris, who got a tighter hold on her uncle. "No!" she said. "Want Rory!"

Cash looked down at his wife musingly. "So there."

She laughed, pressing close against him. "All right, Tris," she told her daughter. "Rory, when your arms get tired, bring her back."

"Okay, sis." He went off toward the fenced pasture where horses were grazing.

Harley excused them and drew Sara along with him to the tables where plates of barbecue and beans and rolls were being served up.

"You sure you're all right?" Harley asked, concerned.

Sara nodded. "It was a shock, that's all."

"I don't like that smarmy lawyer," he muttered darkly. "But she and her boss do suit one another. They're both bad company."

Sara didn't answer him. She was remembering the hard look Jared had given Max. He hadn't liked the woman's reaction to Sara. That was comforting. But her face still stung.

The Latin music played by the Mariachi band had everyone who could walk streaming up onto the wooden dance floor Cy had built for the occasion.

Strings of large Japanese lanterns provided light, after the sun went down, and there was a crowd swaying to the rhythm.

Matt Caldwell and his wife, Leslie, were doing a spirited *paso doble* while Cash and Tippy Grier looked on from the sidelines. They exchanged mischievous glances, got up, held hands and moved onto the dance floor.

"Bet you can't do a tango," Cash chided.

Matt gave him a wicked grin. "You lose. Hey, Paco!" he called to the band leader. "Tango!"

The band leader and his band all laughed, stopped playing, measured the rhythm and then sailed into a Tango number that was all fire and passion.

Everybody except the two couples evacuated the dance floor, expecting a real competition.

They got one. It was a duel, and both couples put on their best form for it. As the music built to a crescendo, both couples stopped at the same time, in lingering poses, as the band finished the number.

But it was a draw, as the dancers had figured it would be. They laughed and shook hands as the audience went wild with clapping and cheering.

"Pity we don't have trophies," Cy Parks drawled.

"Next time, we have to have a waltz contest!" Harley called. He'd been studying the dance for months, and he was good at it.

"I learned to waltz in Austria," Cash called to him.

Harley flapped his hand at the police chief.

The music started again, this time a lazy two-step.

Just as Harley turned to take Sara onto the dance floor, he was bypassed.

Jared Cameron lifted Sara gently into his arms, carried her onto the wooden dance platform and eased her to the floor.

"My turn," he said softly, and he smiled in a way that made her heart race.

She slid her free arm around his neck and looked up at him with her breath catching in her throat.

Harley, for one instant, thought about separating them. But when he saw Sara's face, he knew it would be almost a betrayal to interfere. Subdued, he went back to the buffet table for a beer.

"I didn't think you'd be back," Sara said to his chest. He was so much taller that her head barely came to his chin.

His big, warm hand contracted around hers. "Didn't you?" He tilted her chin up so that he could see her cheek. "At least it isn't bruised," he added quietly. "I've never wanted so badly to manhandle a woman. Max needs to take some classes in anger management."

"She thought I was laughing at her."

"Tony explained it." His hand tightened. "You keep your distance from Tony," he added firmly. "He's not what he seems to be. He could hurt you."

"He would never lift a hand to me," she protested at once.

He stopped dancing for an instant and looked down into her wide eyes. "I don't mean physically."

131

She frowned. "He's very sweet to me."

He started dancing again. "You remind him of his sister."

"Yes. He said she died."

He made a slow turn, one that drew her very close to his hard-muscled body and made her tingle all over. "Tony has issues you're better off not knowing about."

"Cy Parks knows both of you."

"I've lived here several weeks," he said carelessly.

"That isn't what I mean."

He raised an eyebrow. "I've known Cy for a while."

She was really curious now. Most people knew that Cy Parks, Eb Scott and Micah Steele had been professional mercenaries, soldiers of fortune, before they settled down in Jacobsville. She knew next to nothing about Jared Cameron. She wondered what secrets he was keeping.

He saw that curiosity in her eyes and just smiled. "Never you mind," he told her, drawing her closer. "I don't plan to waste the evening with walks down memory lane. I'm much more interested," he added huskily, "in making new memories."

His hand slid gently up and down her spine in sensuous little forays that made her feel boneless. It worried her that she didn't want to protest the near intimacy of his hold. If he ever turned up the heat, she knew she wouldn't be able to resist him. She couldn't help but remember what Max had told her about Jared's easy conquests and his indifference to them afterward.

"I had Tony drive Max to the airport," he said after a minute.

Her heart skipped. "She's gone?"

"Yes. She's gone." He didn't mention the vicious things Max had to say about Sara and Jared's interest in her, or the threat he used to get her out of town. Tony wasn't too keen on leaving Jared alone while he escorted the lawyer to the airport, either. It had been a battle.

"Is Tony coming over, then?" she asked.

He stiffened. "Yes," he said, but he didn't sound happy about it. "I meant what I said. You don't need to start looking at Tony as a prom date."

"I didn't go to the prom," she said absently. "And it's not your business who I look at. I came with Harley," she added firmly.

He drew back so that he could see her eyes. "And you're going home with me," he said softly.

How she wished that her excitement hadn't shown when he said that. She couldn't walk off with another man when Harley had brought her here. It would have been unthinkable . . .

"Sara," Harley said from beside them, grimacing, "I've got something to do for the boss. It can't wait."

"I'll drive her home," Jared told the younger man. "No problem."

"Sara, is that all right with you?" Harley asked gently.

She nodded. "It's okay. What is it? Or can't you say?"

Harley shrugged. "I really can't," he replied. He forced a smile. "We'll do this again, Sara."

She smiled back. "Of course."

He nodded to Jared and walked off toward the parking lot, looking forlorn even from behind.

Jared was smiling.

Sara frowned. "Did you have anything to do with that?"

"You mean, did I ask Cy to occupy Harley so that I could take you home? Of course I did. I don't like competition."

She was gaping. "Excuse me?"

His arm contracted. His eyes were strangely darkened as he met her own. "I'm possessive," he said softly. "Territorial."

"About . . . me?" she asked, unbelieving.

"Of course about you," he muttered.

"But Max is beautiful," she began.

"Max is the past," he said bluntly. "She knows it."

That was thrilling. Exciting. Her whole face lit up. He was serious!

He stopped dancing and traced her mouth with a long forefinger, teasing her lips apart in a sensuous tension that grew by the second. "You're tired," he whispered. "You've done too much. You need to go home, and I have to take you because Harley left early."

She nodded, wordless.

He caught her by the hand and tugged her to Cy and Lisa. They said their goodbyes. Jared asked Cy to tell

Tony where he'd gone. He put Sara in the Jaguar, buckled her up and revved off toward her small house.

They didn't exchange a single word during the short drive. The tension between them was so thick it was almost tangible. Sara felt hot all over. The feel of Jared so close to her had removed all her inhibitions. She couldn't think past wanting to kiss him until her mouth hurt.

He cut off the engine in front of her house and turned to her. "We've reached the point of no return," he said curtly. "Either we go ahead, or we stop seeing each other. I'm too old to stop at kisses."

She stared at him helplessly, all her upbringing urging her to tell him to leave, to go inside by herself. All her life, she'd done the right thing, the safe thing. But she loved this man. If she said the wrong words now, she knew she'd never be in his arms again. The thought was torture. Then she caught herself. She was being overly worried. He wanted to do some heavy petting. Of course. He wasn't a kiss-at-the-front-door sort of man. And if things got too hot, well, she'd just find an excuse to get up. Easy.

He got out of the car, opened her door and locked the sleek vehicle before he followed Sara up onto her porch. Nervously she unlocked the door and went inside. She reached for the light switch, but he was right behind her. He stayed the movement, locked the dead bolt and suddenly swept her up into his arms and brought his mouth down on her soft lips.

The sofa was only a few feet away. It was long and wide, just right for two people to lie on. Sara felt his weight with a sense of destiny. It was the most glorious thing she'd ever felt, all that hard, warm muscle down the length of her body. She seemed to throb like her own runaway heartbeat while Jared made a midnight snack of her mouth.

Before long, she was as anxious as he was to have her blouse and bra out of the way so that his hands, and then his mouth, could explore the softness of her warm skin. By the time he slid his hands under her skirt and against her bare legs, she was shivering all over.

She felt his body vibrate, as if he was as electrified as she was. He whispered something under his breath that she didn't understand. Apparently it wasn't too important, because only seconds later, she felt him against her in a way that was as new as it was frightening.

She started to protest, but it was already too late. His mouth ground into hers as his body suddenly invaded the most secret place of her own. The delicious sensations she felt when they began were now absent as she felt him insistent and demanding, his big hand under her hips, holding them steady as he pushed down hard. He groaned as he felt the soft barrier give. His control was gone at once. He drove for fulfillment; abstinence and too many beers had robbed him of self-control. He felt the rush of pleasure like a hot wave over his body, leaving him to shudder in a tense arch that was like rain after the baking desert.

When he regained his control, he felt her trying to get away from the crush of his body. He was aware of broken sobs. Trembling. Audible misery.

He lifted his head. He couldn't see her in the darkness of the room, but his hand touched her face and felt the wetness.

"Please," she sobbed, pushing at his chest.

He was shocked at his lapse. He hadn't really meant to go this far, not the first time they were intimate. But it was too late now. He moved away, fastening his slacks. He heard her move, heard fabric against skin. At least she'd stopped crying.

"I'll get the light," he said gruffly.

"No!" She was standing now. "No," she added in a more controlled tone. "Please don't."

"Why not?" He moved closer to her. "We made love. What's so horrible about it?"

She was shivering with self-revulsion. "Please go," she whispered.

"Sara . . ."

"Please!" she sobbed.

He drew in an angry breath. "Small town girls and their damned hang-ups," he muttered. "What now? Do you think you'll go to hell for sleeping with a man you haven't married?"

It was so close to what she'd been taught all her life, that she didn't even bother to reply.

"I don't believe this!" he raged. "I can't be the first

137

man to—" He stopped dead, remembering the barrier that he'd dealt with. "I was the first," he said slowly. "Wasn't I, Sara?"

"Please go," she pleaded tearfully.

He drew in a long breath. "Tell me you're on birth control," he demanded.

"I never needed to be," she bit off.

"Great!" he burst out, furious. "That's just great! And you see me as a meal ticket, don't you? If I made you pregnant, you'll have a free ride for life! Except you won't," he added coldly. "I don't want children ever again. You'll have a termination or I'll take you to court and show everyone who lives here how mercenary you are!"

He was talking about a possibility she hadn't even considered. She'd tried to stop him. Why did he expect every woman to be prepared for sex? Was that the way people thought in big cities? Were they all prepared, all the time?

"Don't worry," she said through her teeth. "I promise you, there won't be any horrible consequences. Now will you please go home?"

He started for the door, still furious. But he paused with it open and looked back toward her. "I didn't mean to hurt you," he said uncomfortably.

She laughed hollowly. "My whole life has been nothing except pain. Why should this be any different?"

She turned and went into a room down the hall, closed the door and audibly locked it.

He left, frowning, curious about the remark. He didn't want to think about how much he'd hurt her. He honestly hadn't planned to seduce her, but she wouldn't believe him. She was hurt and shocked and outraged. Probably she'd been taught that premarital sex was a sin, and now she was going to punish herself for falling victim to demon lust.

He turned the lock on her door so that it would engage when he went outside and pulled the door shut.

He stood on the porch, feeling the cool breeze touch his sweaty face, cooling him. He'd never lost control like that in his life. He was furious at himself.

While he was debating his next move, the ranch truck pulled up beside his car. Tony leaned out the window.

"She okay?" he asked his boss.

"She's fine," Jared lied, unlocking the Jaguar. "Let's go home. I want a drink. It's been a damned long day."

"You can say that again," Tony replied. "You won't believe the hell Max raised at the airport."

He'd believe it, he thought. His whole evening had gone from bad to worse, and he wasn't about to tell Tony any of the details. Two women in his life, and he couldn't deal with either of them. He wished that this whole charade was over.

Eight

Sara didn't sleep at all. She took a shower and changed into a clean nightgown. Then she sat in front of her mirror and looked at the fallen woman there. Her grandfather would be ashamed of her. So would her father. They hadn't raised her to be careless with her morals.

She wasn't sure what to do. She knew there was a morning after pill, but she'd have to go to a doctor she knew to ask for it. Everybody in town would know what she'd been doing. The shame was too great for the risk. But what if she conceived? She was only at the beginning of her cycle. Wasn't that a bad time to get pregnant? But some women weren't regular. She wasn't. Would that make a big difference?

Jared hadn't even asked first. He'd taken what he wanted. Maybe she'd done something to make him think she was willing. She should have told him in the car that she was innocent. She'd thought he meant that he wanted to have a nice petting session in her house, not that he expected her to go the whole way with him. Had he thought she was agreeing to sex?

She was sickened by her lack of protest. It had been so sweet to lie in his arms and feel him wanting her. Nobody had ever wanted Sara, not in that way. Her grandfather had cherished her, but she'd been in such a condition when she and her mother first came home from overseas that she wasn't really expected to live in the first place. The group that had sponsored the family's trip had been kind enough to arrange for a medical flight back to Texas for Sara. As a result of her injuries, she had slight brain damage. People who knew her were aware of it. They never made fun of her when she couldn't match socks or clothes, when she forgot little things as soon as she learned them. She had trouble remembering much of the past as well. The doctors had said she was very smart and that she would be able to compensate. But now she wasn't so sure.

Maybe, she comforted herself, nothing would happen. She really hadn't enjoyed what Jared had done to her. Didn't that mean she wouldn't conceive?

She should have read more books, she told herself firmly. She knew too little about her own body, or what men and women did in the dark. At least she knew now what women had been talking about in whispers all her life. Sex was painful and quickly over with. It was only fun for men. Women endured it to have children. Now she knew that she'd never want it again. She knew the truth.

She went to bed. For the first time in years, though, she didn't have nightmares.

Jared felt guilty all day. He was shocked at his loss of control. He was sorry for the things he'd said to Sara, but she should have told him up-front that she had no experience of men. Most women knew how to take care of themselves in intimate situations. If he'd known Sara was completely innocent, he'd have used something and he wouldn't have hurt her so much.

He laughed coldly. Sure he would have. He hadn't had control of himself for those few, electrifying minutes on her sofa. He'd wanted her so much that he couldn't contain it.

Tony hadn't said anything to him about it, but he kept looking at Jared as if he suspected something. It didn't help to remember how fond Tony was getting of Sara. Sara liked Tony, too.

"You aren't yourself today," Tony commented at lunch, for which they had a nice paella that he'd concocted.

Jared moved restlessly, but he didn't reply.

"Max didn't leave town."

That got his boss's attention. "What?!"

Tony compressed his lips. "She's upstairs."

"I told you to take her to the airport!"

"I did," Tony said shortly. "But short of bodily carrying her onto the plane, I couldn't think of a way to get her out of the terminal."

Jared almost exploded. Just as he started to speak, Max lounged into the dining room in a gray silk pantsuit.

"Lunch? I'm starved."

"I told you to leave," Jared shot at her.

"You didn't mean it," she said complacently. "You're always throwing me out. Then the next day you call to apologize and ask me back again. I saved you the steps in between."

She was right, and Jared hated knowing it. She helped herself to paella and coffee. Nobody said anything else at the table.

Jared wasn't a drinker. He hardly ever touched alcohol. But remembering what he'd done with Sara sent him to a liquor bottle. Halfway through the afternoon, he was well on his way to staggering.

Max cornered Jared in his study, surprised at the amount of whiskey he was consuming. It had to be something rough, she thought. He hadn't had this much to drink since his daughter's death. "Something's gone wrong, hasn't it? Come on," she coaxed. "Tell me."

He glared at her. "I can handle this myself."

"Handle what?" She pursed her lips. She knew him very well. There was a pattern to his behavior that she recognized. A new woman. The hunt. The seduction. Then the need to extricate himself from the woman. "Don't tell me," she purred. "You let that hick girl seduce you, didn't you?"

He looked shocked.

"I thought so," she continued. "It was easy to see that she was after you. She watched every move you made. She wore seductive clothes. She did everything except wear a sign to show you that she was willing. No man could have resisted her."

She made him feel less guilty. She was right. It was Sara's fault. He'd been seduced, not the reverse. The alcohol helped him see the truth.

She saw the wheels turning in his mind. "And now you're worried about consequences."

He gave it away without knowing.

She nodded. "Don't worry. I'll take care of everything. You just attend to your current situation and leave it to me."

"Don't hurt her," he said as an afterthought.

"That's a joke. I won't have to."

"Okay." He went to find Tony. He felt a weight lifted from his shoulders. It would be all right. If Tony noticed that his boss was half lit, he was kind enough not to say anything about it.

Sara was back at work on Monday morning, feeling guilty and ashamed, as if what had happened showed on her face.

"Bad weekend?" Dee asked gently. "We all have them, from time to time."

"I went to the barbecue at the Parks's place," she replied. "The food was great."

Dee grinned. "Did Harley have a good time, too?"

"Harley had to go run an errand for his boss just after the dancing started," Sara said sadly. Harley would have saved her if Cy hadn't separated him from Sara.

"Mmm-hmm," Dee murmured.

Something in her tone disturbed Sara. She glanced at her boss. "What?"

"Did you know that Jared and Cy Parks grew up in the same town?"

Sara dropped the stapler she was holding and scrambled to pick it up again. "How do you know?"

"My cousin works for Cy on his ranch. He knows all the gossip. Yes, Cy had a place in Montana, and so did Jared Cameron." She stopped putting used books into boxes for resale. "Jared asked Cy to remove Harley from the field," she added.

Sara had always liked Cy Parks, until now. But he couldn't have known what a near-tragedy he'd contributed to. He probably thought Jared was seriously interested in Sara. According to Max, Jared was never seriously interested in any woman. Especially, she recalled sickly, once he'd had her. Her eyes closed in misery.

"Harley was topping cotton he was so mad," Dee continued. "He almost quit his job. He said you were a babe in the woods and Jared was a wolf in disguise."

"Jared was a perfect gentleman," Sara lied, and made it look convincing.

Dee stared at her for a minute and then visibly relaxed. "Thank goodness. I was worried . . . silly of me. I have to run to the bank to get some change for the drawer. Want coffee from the doughnut place?"

"Yes, please, black. No cream or sugar."

"That's new. You're sure?"

"I'm getting back to the basics, even in coffee. I'll hold down the fort."

Dee smiled gently. "Okay."

After Dee left, Sara felt as if the world was collapsing around her. It was a crisis that compared in intensity only to that episode in her past. She'd survived that, she reminded herself. She could survive anything, after that.

But minutes later, Max parked one of the ranch trucks outside the bookstore and strolled in, looking smug and arrogant. "Jared sent me," she said curtly. She took out an envelope and handed it to Sara. "It's a check for ten thousand dollars. He said there had better not be any complications from what happened Saturday night." She nodded toward the envelope. "There's more than enough in there to pay for a termination. And if it's not necessary, then you've still got a nest egg for the foreseeable future. Jared won't be here much longer."

"Won't . . . be here," Sara stammered, shocked by the unfolding nightmare.

"He's been down here waiting for the authorities to get their hands on three illegal aliens who came up from South America to kidnap Jared and hold him for ransom."

"Ransom?"

Max pulled a magazine from her briefcase. It was a national financial journal. There, on the front cover, was Jared Cameron. The story inside was revealed in a sentence: Oil magnate target of terrorists after fire-fight at South American pipeline . . .

Sara gasped.

"You can keep it," Max said easily. "To remember him by."

"But why did he come here?" Sara asked blankly.

"Because some of the team of mercenaries that helped him destroy the original terrorist cell that targeted his oil pipeline two years ago live here," she replied. "The survivors aren't willing to give up. They figure if they can nab Jared, they'll recoup what they lost when they failed to hold on to his oil pipeline in South America. They demanded millions for it, and he sent in mercenaries instead. He pulled out when the oil companies were nationalized, but the terrorists still want the money. Now they want revenge as well. They were just apprehended today near Victoria."

"Then he's safe," Sara said dully.

"He is. And he can go down to Cancún with me for a long holiday," she added. "His headquarters is in Oklahoma, but he has another house in Billings, Montana, and vacation homes all over the world. He's worth millions. The terrorists knew that his corporation would pay any amount of money to get him back. He's something of a financial genius." Her eyes narrowed as she smiled. "Hardly a match for a little bookseller in outback Texas, is he?"

Sara just looked at her, with the anguish she couldn't hide all over her face.

Max's expression hardened. "You'd better realize that he means business. If you turn up pregnant, you'd better get a termination. You don't want to know what he could do to you and your reputation."

Sara didn't answer her. She couldn't. She just stared.

Max shrugged. "You've been warned." She stopped at the doorway. "You shouldn't look so tragic. Women have fought their way into his bed for years."

"What for?" Sara asked with deliberate scorn.

Max looked as if she'd been doused with water. "You don't mean that you didn't enjoy . . . ?"

"I'd rather stay single for the rest of my life than go through that again, ever," Sara said with a sob in her voice.

Something in Max that had been buried for a decade sat up and shivered. She searched for the right words. "You've never . . . ?"

Sara swallowed hard. "My grandfather said that women who give their bodies cheaply are bound for purgatory."

Max's thin eyebrows pulled together. "Sara," she began hesitantly, "how old are you?"

"What does that have to do with . . . ?"

"How old are you?"

Sara swallowed. "Nineteen."

Max felt the blood going out of her face. She was using a cannon to shoot a bird. She drew in a long breath. Well, at least it hadn't been statutory rape. But she was sure Jared didn't know how old this child was. He'd never have touched her.

"I'm sorry," Max told her. "I'm really sorry."

She turned and went out the door.

Sara dried her tears and went back to straightening the books on their shelves. Jared was a multimillion-aire who owned an oil corporation and he was only here at the ranch to set a trap for the terrorists who wanted him for ransom. Sara had thought he was here forever. When he held her close and kissed her, she thought he wanted her forever. She was wrong on both counts. He could buy as many women as he wanted. Sara wasn't even in the running, except that he'd wanted her. Or, maybe he'd just wanted a woman and she was handy. She really did need to grow up.

Max was solemn and quiet when she went back to the ranch. Jared noticed.

"What's wrong?" he asked.

She looked up at him. "She's nineteen, Jared."

He had to sit down. Nothing had ever hit him quite so hard.

She sat down across from him in an armchair. "I told her what was necessary . . ."

"You what?" he asked, aghast.

She held up a hand. "Being kind to her isn't an option. What if she decided to accuse you of forcing her? You could lose millions. Your reputation would be in ashes. What sort of life would it be for a child, if she had one, living in this small town asylum with a mother who barely made minimum wage and could hardly afford to clothe her?"

Jared wasn't thinking about money. He was remembering the throb in Sara's voice in the darkness. She hadn't been leading him on. She hadn't realized what he meant. She didn't know that she

149

was agreeing to have sex with him. And she was nineteen years old. He felt guilt like a rush of hot acid in his gut.

"When are we going to Cancún?" Max asked, to divert him.

He turned and looked at her, but he didn't see her. "I haven't thought about it."

"A few days on the beach would do you good," she coaxed. "You can put this place behind you."

He was staring at her. "Why Cancún?" he asked.

She hesitated. "It's got lovely beaches. There are Mayan ruins nearby."

His eyes had narrowed. "You'd better come clean."

She frowned. "I'm not doing anything dishonest," she said. "There's a consortium that handles pharmaceuticals. They want to invest in our corporation."

"Name them."

She frowned more. "Well, I don't really have just one name. They call themselves the Reconquistas."

"When did you speak with them?"

"Last week. Why?"

"Law enforcement just apprehended three terrorists in Victoria, heading this way," he said furiously. "And you don't know why?"

She looked stunned. "You can't mean . . . !"

"They're part of the consortium that smuggles narcotics, Max," he told her flatly. "If you'd come to me in the first place, I would have told you. But you were seeing dollar signs, weren't you?"

She flushed. "It never hurts to make more money."

"It never hurts to fire people, either," he said pointedly. "You'd better start looking for another job."

"You're not serious," she laughed. "You fire me all the time, but you always call me back."

He looked resolute. "Not this time," he said in a cold tone. "You've done enough damage."

"Me?" She stood up, fuming. "I've done enough damage? What would you call seducing a nineteen-year-old virgin?"

The last word drifted away as she noticed Tony standing fixed in the doorway, with eyes that promised mayhem.

Jared saw him and grimaced.

Tony marched right up to him. "Is it true?" he demanded.

Jared couldn't even find the words.

"That sweet woman," Tony said coldly, "who never hurt anybody, after the tragedy of her past almost destroyed her, and here you come to put the last nail in her coffin!"

"What do you mean, the tragedy of her past?" Jared asked.

Tony didn't reply. He looked more dangerous at that moment than Jared had ever seen before. "I'll never tell you. And the minute this standoff ends, I'm through. I won't work for a man like you."

He turned on his heel and went right back to the kitchen.

Max swallowed the hurt. She and Tony had both hit rock bottom, it seemed. "Well, it looks like you and your conscience will have a long time to get to know each other, doesn't it?"

She stopped by the kitchen to ask Tony to drive her to the airport. He agreed curtly. Jared went back into his study and slammed the door. He'd never felt so ashamed in his life.

The next morning, when Sara went to work, she noticed a strange beat-up van in the parking lot. It had been there just as she drove out of the parking lot the day before. In fact, it had pulled in just after Max walked into the bookstore. Sara hadn't seen anybody in it the day before, and she didn't see any people in it now. Maybe it broke down there and the owner had left it until he could get a mechanic to tow it. She went into the bookstore.

"Hi, Dee," she called.

Dee smiled. "Hi, yourself. I'm off to the bank. Want coffee?"

"I'd love it."

"I'll pick us up a doughnut apiece, too." She stopped at the door. "That old van's still there."

"Maybe it broke down," Sara murmured.

"I'm amazed anyone would risk driving it in the first place," Dee chuckled. "I'll be quick."

"Okay."

She'd no sooner driven away than three foreign-looking men walked into the bookstore. They glanced at Sara and nodded before they walked down the aisles, one of them peering into Dee's open office.

152

Sara didn't usually have premonitions, but she felt something odd about the men. She remembered what Max had said about terrorists. These three were tall and swarthy and disreputable-looking. They were wearing jeans and T-shirts, and they had very prominent muscles. She was in the bookstore alone, with no weapons except the pocketknife she used to open boxes with. She wouldn't stand a chance against even one of them, much less three, despite Chief Grier's handy self-defense for women course. She could scream, of course, but the bookstore was temporarily the only business in the strip mall.

They might have been arrested in Victoria, but it was obvious that they'd made bail. She knew the look of the people who lived in her area. These three were from overseas. And she didn't need a program to know why they were in town. They were after Jared. Max had come to the bookstore in a ranch pickup and had a solemn conversation with a woman. They might have had high-tech listening devices. If they knew who Max was, and they'd overheard what she said to Sara, maybe they figured Sara was a softer target than Jared, with his bodyguard.

She pretended not to see them, while her mind worried over possible courses of action. There was one. It was a long shot. If she stabbed herself with the pocketknife and they could see blood, and she pretended to be unconscious and tried to look dead, they might be startled into leaving. It would be risky to carry a wounded woman off for ransom, wouldn't it? Especially if she looked as if she were dying . . . it would slow everything down.

I'm probably crazy, she told herself. They're just tourists or ranch hands searching for something to read. Right, she added, and that's why they're looking outside to make sure nobody's coming and heading straight for me!

She knew where the appendicitis incision was. It was her best hope of missing any essential organs. They came around the counter, towering over her.

"You come with us," one of the men said in accented English. "We see you with the lawyer. You are Cameron's woman. He will pay for you."

"I am nobody's woman. I will die before I go with you!" she said, and, giving up a silent prayer, she jabbed the pocketknife into the incision, through her blouse. "Oooh!" she cried, because it did hurt.

She crumpled to the floor with blood on her hands and shirt. She sighed heavily and held her breath. She looked dead.

The men hesitated. They'd planned well, and now their hostage had committed suicide right in front of them!

While they hesitated, Harley Fowler got out of his truck and headed for the bookstore. He was wearing a sidearm, a six-gun that he carried when he was working fence lines, in case he encountered a rattler or some other dangerous animal. The men made a quick decision. They ran for it. They ran so fast that they almost knocked Harley down in the process.

Harley didn't understand why three men were running for the van. Then he thought about robbery. Sara and Dee were here alone. He darted into the bookstore.

Sara was on the floor, blood pouring from her side. She looked up at Harley, gasping for breath. "It worked," she mumbled. "I hurt myself, though. Can you call 911 please?"

He grimaced as he saw the blood. "Yes, I can." He flipped out his cell phone and pushed in the code, holding it to his ear with his shoulder as he pulled Sara's shirt aside and looked at the wound.

He put pressure on it to stop the bleeding and spoke into the cell phone between his shoulder and his ear. He had an ambulance sent to the bookstore. He managed to hold one hand on her wound and close the phone with the other and slide it back into his pocket.

"You'll be all right, Sara," he told her. "Any man who'd do this to a woman should be shot! I should have stopped them!"

"They didn't do it, Harley, I did," she said weakly. "They were going to kidnap me. They thought Jared Cameron would pay ransom for me. What a joke!"

"Why would they think that?"

"His lawyer, Max, came to buy me off yesterday," she said miserably. "They must have followed her here."

"You aren't making sense."

The wound hurt. She moved and flinched. "Look at

the magazine on the counter, Harley," she told him. "You'll see."

"When the paramedics get here, I will," he replied, but he didn't move his hands. He didn't dare.

Dee and the ambulance arrived at the same time. She ran into the store, red-faced and fearful.

"Oh, my goodness!" she exclaimed. "Sara!"

"Three men. They were in that old van, I think," she told Dee. "They were going to kidnap me for ransom."

"Ransom? Dear, you must be feverish . . ."

Harley picked up the magazine and looked at it, frowning as he handed it to Dee.

They exchanged a worried glance.

The paramedics loaded Sara on the gurney.

"I'll go with her," Harley said. "Dee, you'd better call Cash Grier, in case they come back."

"I'll do it right now." She picked up the store phone.

"I'll be all right. Honest," Sara assured Harley.

He didn't answer. He was too worried.

The wound wasn't bad. Dr. Coltrain had to sew her up. He did it, after giving her a local anesthetic, shaking his head. "Couldn't you have dialed 911?" he asked.

"I'd never have made it to the phone. There were three of them, heavily muscled, with accents, and not Spanish ones. I heard accents like that in Africa," she whispered.

"Why were they after you?" he asked.

"They were going to take me for ransom."

"Oh. Who do you know with that kind of money?" Coltrain teased.

"They followed Jared Cameron's lawyer into the bookstore," she murmured, feeling drowsy now that the excitement was all over. "I guess they thought I had a connection to him that they could exploit. There's an article about him in the new financial magazine. His photo's on the cover. He's down here trying to avoid being kidnapped by South American terrorists who made a try for his oil pipeline."

"The excitement of living in Jacobsville, Texas," he replied as he stitched her up. "When I was a kid, this place was like the end of the world. Never any excitement."

"Maybe he'll go away and we'll get back to normal."

He only mumbled.

Sara was sitting up on the examination table when Cash Grier walked in.

"Harley said three men attacked you in the bookstore," he said without preamble. He looked solemn. "Three prisoners escaped from the Victoria jail yesterday about noon. They were Arabic, according to the police chief up there. At least, they spoke what sounded to him like Arabic."

"Yes," she replied. "They were in a ratty old van. They followed Jared Cameron's lawyer to the bookstore in one of the ranch trucks. They thought I was important to Mr. Cameron. What a joke!"

He didn't laugh. "Did they say anything to you?"

"Only that they thought I had a connection to him. They must be really desperate for a hostage."

"Did one of them stab you?" he asked.

She grimaced. "You aren't going to believe this."

"Try me."

"I stabbed myself. I made them think I was committing suicide. They hesitated when I fell on the floor and pretended to be dead. Then Harley showed up and they cut their losses and ran for it. Good thing Harley was wearing his .45 on his hip today!" she added. "He always does when he rides fence lines."

Cash's dark eyebrows arched and he smiled gently. "Well, aren't you the mistress of improvisation?" he said with respect.

She grinned. "It seemed the only chance I had. There were three of them. You always said there was no shame in running if you were up against impossible odds."

"Yes, I did. You spooked them, I gather."

"Want to hire me?" she asked saucily. "You can teach me how to shoot a gun and next time I won't have to resort to stabbing myself. I can shoot them instead."

"We've put out a BOLO on the van," Cash assured her.

"It will stick out," she said. "It really is ratty."

Harley stuck his head in the door. "How are you?"

She smiled. "Dr. Coltrain sewed me back up. I'm fine."

"You couldn't have screamed?" he asked.

"Who would have heard me?" she retorted. "We're the only business left in the strip mall."

"She has a point," Cash told the younger man.

Just then, his radio beeped. He talked into the radio mike on his shoulder. "Grier."

"We got them," Assistant Chief Judd Dunn told him. "We're bringing them in now."

"On my way," Cash replied. "Clear."

He turned to Sara, grinning. "And that's a nice day's work. Stop stabbing yourself," he added firmly. "I'm sure there's a law against attempted suicide."

"Never again. I promise," she assured him.

He winked and left. Harley moved into the cubicle and held Sara's hand.

"What a relief to find you in one piece," he said gently.

Sara smiled at him. He wasn't the only person who was relieved.

There was a terrible commotion in the corridor. Seconds later, Tony the Dancer walked into the cubicle.

Nine

Tony glanced at Harley, who was holding Sara's hand in his.

"I heard those three assassins went after you," Tony told her, worried. "They followed Max, didn't they?"

"I think they did," she admitted. "But how did they know her?"

"Our Web site mentions all the people who work for the corporation," he replied. "I'm sure the would-be kidnappers are computer literate. Most terrorists are these days. You okay?"

She smiled at him. She nodded.

"What did they do to you?" he asked, noting the dried blood on her blouse.

"They didn't do anything. I stabbed myself where I had the appendectomy and played dead on the floor. They didn't want a dying hostage, I figured. Then Harley showed up with his .45 and spooked them while they were deciding what to do about me. They ran. Chief Grier said his men just stopped them and they're under arrest."

Tony let out a breath. He glanced at Harley and smiled. "You do look like a gunslinger," he said.

Harley chuckled. "I never get any practice on living targets," he said. "Pity they ran."

"Wasn't it just?" Sara murmured. She grimaced.

Copper Coltrain came back into the cubicle, raising his eyebrows at the newcomer.

"This is Tony Danzetta," Sara introduced him. "He works for Mr. Cameron."

Coltrain nodded. So did Tony.

Harley checked his watch. "Damn! Sara, I was on my way to pick up some butane and fencing for Mr. Parks when I stopped by the bookstore for a minute to see you. I've got to go."

"Could you call Dee and tell her I'll be there as soon as Dr. Coltrain releases me," she began.

"In a pig's eye you will," Coltrain snapped, his red hair seemed to flare up. "You'll go home and stay in bed for two days. You'll start an antibiotic as well, to protect against that wound getting infected." He hesitated. "You don't need to be on your own."

"Chief Grier and his men have the would-be kidnappers in custody," she repeated.

"Sara, that isn't what I mean," he replied.

"She won't be alone," Tony said quietly. "I'll take her home and get the prescription filled. Then I'll take care of her until she's well."

"But, your boss," Sara began.

"I'm quitting today," he returned, avoiding her eyes. "If they've got the kidnappers, he won't need me. He doesn't need protection anymore. If he does, he can hire somebody else. He's rich enough."

Sara sensed a confrontation, and she was sure she didn't want to know why Tony had quit. She was almost certain it had something to do with her.

She flushed scarlet as she considered what Tony might have found out from Max.

Coltrain saw the flush and Tony's tight lips and drew a conclusion. "Mr. Danzetta, I need to take one more look at the incision. Will you wait outside, please? You, too, Harley."

"I'm just going. Get better, Sara," Harley said softly, smiling.

"I'll do my best. Thanks for what you did."

"It wasn't much. See you."

"I'll be right outside," Tony added, following Harley out into the hall.

Coltrain closed the door of the cubicle. His eyes were quiet and intense. "You don't have to say it. I read faces very well. What do you want to do?"

She started to deny it. She knew better. Coltrain was a force of nature. "I can't kill an ant," she said.

He scowled. "Who asked you to?"

She pulled the envelope with the check out of her pocket and handed it to him, nodding when he started to open it.

Tony the Dancer heard the curses outside in the hall. He opened the door and went back in, daring the doctor to throw him out.

"What?" he asked.

Coltrain, red in the face with bad temper, handed him the envelope.

He cursed as darkly as the doctor had. "A firefight in Africa that damned near killed her, and now this," he muttered.

Sara and the doctor gaped at him.

He cleared his throat. He looked at Sara. "You

don't remember me, do you?" he asked.

She shook her head, feeling again the sadness that came with remembering her past.

Tony moved a step closer and stuck his hands in his pockets. "I was with a group of American mercs who were fighting to restore the rightful government in the province where your parents were mission-aries," he said quietly. "We'd just driven into town, chasing after a rebel group that killed two of our men. We saw the explosion. And we found you and your parents."

She stared at him, trying to reconcile her memories. "Yes. Some mercenaries buried my . . . my father," she said huskily. "And one of them carried me to a truck and got me and my mother to safety, to the mission headquarters."

"That was me, Sara," Tony replied quietly.

She smiled sadly. She hadn't recognized him. But then, she couldn't remember much of that long-ago life. "I lost some of my long-term memory. I can't quite match colors, and I forget names . . ."

"You're smart, though," Tony replied. "It doesn't show. Honest."

Coltrain drew in a long breath. "It's a small world, isn't it?" he asked.

Tony nodded. "Cy Parks was in another group of mercs, working with us. He walked right into the gunfire of a machine nest and took it out. One of the men who died had set the explosion in the mission that killed Sara's father and injured her."

Sara was spellbound. "I never knew," she said softly.

"You never needed to," Tony told her. He looked at Coltrain. "When can you tell if she's pregnant?"

Sara gasped.

Coltrain took it as a matter of course. "In a couple of weeks," he replied. "Maybe three. I could do a blood test now, but we might get a false positive. You need to shoot your damned boss," he added without missing a beat.

"I'm tempted," Tony said curtly. "But it's too late now. What's done is done. I'll take care of her, no matter what."

Sara fought tears and lost.

Tony pulled her face to his shoulder and held it there while she cried. "Now, now," he said gently. "It's all over. Everything's going to be fine."

Coltrain clapped Tony on the shoulder. "I'll write the prescriptions for an antibiotic and some pain medication. You can make sure she takes it properly."

"You bet I will," Tony replied.

Sara felt like royalty. Tony was a wonder. He cleaned the place until it shined like a new penny, rearranged her uncoordinated shelves in the kitchen and made dinner. He also doled out pills and did the laundry.

Afterward, he called Dee and gave her a progress report.

Sara was aghast when he told her, late that night. "You told her you were staying with me?" she asked.

He glowered at her. "At least Dee doesn't have a dirty mind," he informed her.

"I do not have a dirty mind," she protested.

He drew the covers up over her, in the plain, discreet pajamas she was wearing. "I want to tell you a story," he said, sitting down on the edge of the bed beside her. His dark eyes were quiet and sad. "I had a sister, who was three years younger than me. We lived in foster care. Our old man drank and knocked us around a lot. Our mother was long dead. They took us away from the old man and we shuttled from foster home to foster home, where we were mostly barely tolerated. At one of the homes," he added coldly, "there was an older boy who liked the way my sister looked. I warned him off, but he was persistent and she was flattered that a boy liked her. She was only fourteen, you see." He drew in a long breath and looked down at the floor. "Long story short, he got her pregnant. She was so ashamed, so scared, that she didn't know what to do. The boy found out and told her he'd make her sorry if she didn't get rid of the kid. He wasn't going to be rooked into paying child support for sixteen years because she was too stupid to get the pill and use it."

"What a nasty boy," she muttered.

"She was too ashamed to tell the foster parents what she'd let him do, and too afraid of the boy to have the child. I was moved to another foster home while all this was going on, so she couldn't tell me, either. So she went out one night, after everybody was asleep.

They found her washed up on the riverbank the next afternoon."

"Oh, Tony," she said gently. She touched his arm. "I'm so sorry."

He grimaced. "She was all I had."

She slid her little hand into his big one and smiled at him. "No. I'm your family now," she replied. "You can be my big brother."

He looked down at her with eyes that were suspiciously bright. "Yeah?"

She squeezed his hand. "Yeah."

He drew in a steadying breath. "Well, we'll be part of one amazingly dysfunctional family, if you still consider Jared part of it."

She glared. "He became a stranger when Max handed me that check. And we're not going to let him be in our family anymore, either."

He didn't believe that she'd stopped caring about Jared. She was just hurt. So he smiled and nodded his head. "Suits me."

He squeezed her hand and let it go. "You need to get some sleep," he said, standing. He smiled down at her. "I'll be a better family to you than my ex-boss was," he added coolly. "That's for sure."

The memory of how close she and Jared had become, until the end, made her sad. She'd cared for him more than she wanted to admit. His betrayal was almost more than she could bear.

"Don't brood," Tony said firmly. "It won't change anything. We'll deal with whatever happens."

"I'm not getting rid of a child, if the test comes up positive."

He smiled. "I never thought you would."

"We won't tell him," she muttered. "He can go back to his houses all over the world and have fun with Max."

"Nobody has fun with Max," Tony told her. "She's got a one-track mind. All she thinks about is money."

"That's sad. I mean, it would be nice to have money. But I'm happy living the way I do."

"So am I, kid," he told her. "Money's poor company if it's all you've got."

She smoothed the cover over her belly, wondering. "He loved his little girl," she said out of the blue, and felt sorry for him all over again.

"He did," Tony had to admit. "But he discovered it far too late. Now he's alone and afraid to risk having another child. He'd be vulnerable."

She laid back against the pillows. "Everybody's vulnerable. You can't escape life."

"Yeah," he had to agree. "I know."

She didn't expect to sleep, but she did. It was comforting having Tony down the hall. People would probably gossip about her, but she'd live with it; with the pregnancy, too, if she had to. Her friends wouldn't snub her, and it didn't matter if her enemies did. She frowned. She didn't have enemies. Well, unless you counted that conceited rancher who couldn't take no for an answer.

Tony brought her breakfast and went to work baking them a nice pound cake. But just before lunch, he walked in with her portable phone, his big hand over the mouthpiece.

"Who do you know in New York City?" he asked, curious.

"No one . . . New York? Give me that!" She was almost on fire with excitement as he handed her the phone. She wrenched her newest set of stitches grasping for it and groaned before she spoke into the receiver. "Sara Dobbs," she said at once.

"Miss Dobbs, I'm Daniel Harris, an editor with Mirabella Publishing Company. I wanted to tell you that your story is delightful, and the drawings are exquisite. We'd like to publish your book!"

Sara sat there with dreams coming true. Tears rolled down her cheeks. She fought to find her voice. Yesterday her world had felt as if it were ending. Today . . . today was magic!

"I'd love that," she managed finally, and then listened while he outlined the process that would ensue, including an advance against royalties that would be forthcoming.

Tony lifted his eyebrows while he listened unashamedly to her conversation. She was so animated that he wouldn't have been surprised to see her levitate right up to the ceiling.

She hung up, finally, and handed him back the phone. "They bought my book. They bought my children's book! They're going to publish it! And I get paid!"

He laughed. "Well!"

"I can't believe it!"

"What's this book about?" he asked, curious.

She told him, going into detail about the puppies and their adventures. "I have to call Lisa and tell her. She'll be so thrilled. I'll call Tom Walker, too," she added. "His dog was their grandfather—old Moose, who died just recently."

"I'd love to see this book," Tony replied.

"I just happen to have a copy," she told him, and pointed to the small desk in the corner of her bedroom. "I made a duplicate, in case it got lost in the mail."

He sat beside her and went through the drawings, exclaiming over their beauty. "I never knew anybody who could draw like this," he murmured. "You're really good."

"Thanks, Tony. I'm overwhelmed. I never dreamed it would even sell, and certainly not so quickly."

He glanced at her. "You know, life evens out. Something bad happens, and then you get something good."

"My grandfather used to say that." She leaned back against the pillows. "My mother hated him. He talked my father into the mission to Africa, something he'd always wanted to do, but never could. Mama didn't want to go. She thought Africa was too dangerous, but my grandfather and my father made her feel guilty enough to back down. She blamed Grandad for everything that happened. She went out of her way to embarrass him, to make him pay for Daddy's death." She shook her head. "The only person she really hurt was herself."

"You poor kid," he said gently. "I thought I had a bad life."

"Everybody has a bad life, up to a point," she replied, smiling. "But somehow we survive, and get tougher."

"So we do."

She'd just finished a cup of coffee when the door opened and Jared Cameron stalked in. His face was unshaven. His eyes were bloodshot. He looked worn-out and irritated. He wasn't smiling.

He stood over her, glaring. "Why didn't you call me? Why didn't Tony call me? You were targeted because of me!"

She felt uncomfortable with him, after what had happened. She couldn't meet his eyes. "We didn't think you'd want to know."

He cursed fiercely. "The police chief said the kidnappers followed Max to your bookstore. I didn't send Max to see you!" he raged.

Her sad eyes managed to meet his. "I guess she forged your name on the check, huh?"

He went very still.

That did make her feel a little better, but not much. She pulled the envelope out of the bedside drawer and tossed it to the foot of the bed where he was standing. "You'd better have it back," she said. "I don't take bribes."

His high cheekbones went a ruddy color as he picked it up and looked at it. "Damn Max!" he said under his breath.

"And I'm not having a termination," she added fiercely. "You have no right to try to force me to jeopardize my soul!"

He looked at her as if he didn't understand what she was saying. But slowly it came to him, and he seemed even more ill at ease. "I don't want another child," he bit off.

"Then why didn't you stop?" she demanded hotly.

The flush got worse. "I didn't mean it to go that far," he said curtly. "I swear to God I didn't."

It didn't help much, but it helped a little.

"I thought you were older," he added heavily. "Nineteen years old. Dear God!"

That helped a little more.

He stuck his hands into his pockets. "I fired Max."

"I'm not surprised."

"Which one of those SOBs stabbed you?" he added abruptly.

She blinked. "None of them," she said. "I stabbed myself. It was the only thing I could think of. I was alone and there were three of them. I thought they wouldn't want a dying hostage."

"You did what?" he exploded, horrified.

"I had a pocketknife. I stabbed myself where Dr. Coltrain did the appendectomy. It bled a lot, but I didn't hit anything vital. It was all I could think of."

He winced. "If Max hadn't taken it on herself to

interfere, they'd never have tracked her to you," he said. "I could have choked her when she told me."

"She didn't tell you about the check, I guess?"

"No," he replied curtly. "If she had, she'd never work again. I make a bad enemy."

She knew that already, from personal experience. She studied him quietly. "I thought you were just a comfortably well-off rancher," she said slowly. "That magazine story said you own oil corporations."

He frowned. "What magazine?"

"Max showed it to me," she said. "You were on the cover."

He let out a short breath. "It just keeps getting better and better," he gritted.

Tony came into the room, angry. "How did you get in here?"

"I walked in the front door," Jared shot back. "You should have called me!"

Tony glared at him. "Wouldn't you be lucky if I did?"

Jared glanced from Tony's hard face to Sara's hard face. He grimaced. "It isn't doing your reputation much good to have Tony hanging around here day and night," he said.

"See? He's got a dirty mind, too," Sara told Tony.

"I have not!" Jared gritted. "I hate to see you being gossiped about."

"Then don't listen. It's a small town," she pointed out. "There's usually not much excitement going on around here. Gossip is how we get through life."

Jared seemed to draw inside himself as he looked at Sara. All his regrets were in his green eyes. He glanced at Tony. "Give us a minute, will you?"

If he'd demanded, Tony would have dug in his heels. But it was hard to argue with politeness. He shrugged. "Okay. I'll be in the kitchen, Sara."

"Okay," she replied.

Jared stuck his hands deeper in his pockets and looked down at her. "When will you know for sure?" he asked.

She fought a scarlet flush. "Dr. Coltrain says it's too soon to be sure. Two or three more weeks, I think."

"Damn the luck," he cursed through his set teeth.

She glared at him. "You go right ahead and curse," she said. "But all of this is your fault."

His eyes were sad and full of guilt. She was so young. "I know that, Sara," he said quietly. "It doesn't help much."

She sagged back against the pillows. She didn't know what she was going to do. Her conscience wouldn't let her take the easy way out, although she was pretty sure that he wanted her to.

"Don't torment yourself," he said after a minute. "You did nothing wrong, except trust me. That was a mistake. I haven't had a lot to do with women in the past few months. I just lost it. I'm sorry, if it helps."

It did, a little, but it was too late for an apology to be of much use. "Nobody ever made such a heavy pass at me," she murmured, not meeting his eyes. "I thought you just wanted to kiss me."

"I did," he said heavily. "But kisses lead to other things. I thought you were older, more experienced."

"You wish," she said curtly.

He sighed. "Well, we'll deal with it when we have to," he said after a minute. He looked down at her quietly, his green eyes searching, curious. "I should never have let them talk me into coming here," he told her. "Tony wanted the extra protection that some of his old comrades could provide. I didn't expect to have you drawn into this."

"Neither did I," she said. She stared at her fingers. "I guess it was hard on you, living in a little hick town, with no suitable women around to date."

He made a rough sound in his throat. "Stop that," he said shortly. "You weren't a substitute, Sara."

"Max said you love women until you seduce them, and then you just throw them away," she returned, staring straight at him.

His high cheekbones colored. "Damn Max!"

"If you're filthy rich, I expect you can buy as many women as you want," she continued conversationally.

"I don't buy women," he informed her. "I just don't want to get married."

"I don't think there's much danger of that, with Max carrying payoff checks around to all your girlfriends."

"I told you, I didn't tell Max to do that! It was her idea," he added. "She said she'd handle everything, and I was drunk enough not to care how."

Her eyebrows arched. "Drunk?"

He looked rigid. "You asked me to stop, and I couldn't," he growled. "How do you think I felt? I read the situation wrong and threw my conscience to the wind. Then Max told me how old you were." He winced. "Nineteen. Dear God!"

"Well, I'm not exactly a child," she shot back, growing angry herself. "And I'm no stranger to violence."

"People hit you with books in the bookstore, do they?" he asked, in a condescending, faintly amused tone.

She looked him in the eye. "A rebel paramilitary unit in Sierra Leone tossed a grenade into the clinic where my father was dressing wounds," she replied, watching the shock hit him. "I was standing beside him, holding a bowl of water. I was just ten, it was the only way I was able to help. My father died. I was concussed so badly that I had brain damage. That's why I can't match socks and earrings," she added. "I was right in the path of the grenade. Fragments penetrated my skull. One's still in there," she told him. "They were afraid to try to take it out."

His face was white. Absolutely white. "Why were you there?"

"My grandfather talked my father into doing a stint at missionary work. Dad had been a medic in the army and he was a lay preacher. He and my grandfather forced my mother into going. I begged to go, too. I thought Africa had to be the most exciting place on earth," she added in a dull, quiet tone. "Well, it was exciting, I guess."

"What happened to your mother?"

"She drank herself to death, after she used every low trick she could think of to embarrass my grandfather, to make him pay for Daddy's death. She grew famous locally. It's why I was innocent," she added bitterly. "I was afraid to go out with local boys, because she'd slept with some of them. Everybody thought I was like her. Everybody except Grandad."

Jared winced. "You didn't tell me any of this," he accused.

"We were friends," she replied heavily. "Just friends. I knew you'd never want somebody like me for keeps. I'm nothing like Max, or the women who chase after you. I don't care about money, I don't like diamonds, I'd never fit into high society and I'm brain-damaged. It would never have been my idea to get involved with you physically," she added coldly, "because I knew from the outset that there would be no future in it."

His teeth were grinding together. He'd felt bad before. Now he was sick to his stomach. Somewhere along the road to get rich, he'd lost his way. He had everything he'd ever wanted, but he had no one to share it with. He was alone. He would always be alone, surrounded by women who liked expensive jewelry and travel. And by bodyguards hired to protect him from people who wanted his money enough to risk anything to get it.

"It's going to ruin your reputation, having Tony live here with you," he pointed out.

"What reputation?" she muttered. "Thanks to you, I'm a fallen woman. If I do get pregnant, it's not something I'll be able to hide. Everybody who sees me will know what I've been up to. You'll be off in Las Vegas gambling, or sailing a yacht in the Mediterranean. At least Tony cares about me."

"There are things about Tony that you don't know," he said flatly.

"Yes, and there are things about Tony that you don't know, either," she retorted. "Tony got me to the hospital in time for them to save my life in Africa. I don't remember him, of course. A lot of my childhood was removed along with the damaged tissue in my brain."

His face was almost frozen in place. Nothing had gone right for him since the death of his daughter. He'd destroyed the life of the young woman in that bed. He'd disgraced and shamed himself. He didn't know what to do. But he knew that he needed to do something. He couldn't walk away and let Sara face this alone, not even with Tony for company. He'd have to have a nice talk with Tony, who hadn't bothered to tell him what he knew about Sara. All this misery might have been prevented.

"Don't you have a board meeting or a conference or a yacht race to go to?" Sara asked when he didn't speak. "I'd hate to delay you in any way from your business."

His eyes almost glowed red. He was just about to

open his mouth and let her have it with both barrels when Tony walked in, carrying the phone.

"Sorry, Sara, but it's that guy from New York again," he said, handing it to her.

Jared frowned. "And just who the hell do you know in New York?" he demanded suddenly.

Ten

His own words shocked Jared. He was jealous. He didn't want to be.

Sara, oblivious to his thoughts, was torn between telling Jared to mind his own business and talking to the editor who was going to buy her book.

"Hello?" came a voice from over the telephone.

She put it to her ear. "This is Sara," she said.

Jared glared at her.

"Miss Dobbs? It's Daniel Harris here, at Mirabella Publishing Company."

"Yes, Mr. Harris?"

"I wanted to ask if you could do us a colored drawing of just one of the puppies to use in advertising. Also, we're going to need some ideas for a title. The contract will be on its way to you later this week. You aren't agented, are you?"

"No, I'm not," she said worriedly. "Do I need to be?"

"Of course not. You can have an attorney look over the contract for you, if you have any worries. We're offering you a standard royalty contract, with an advance—" he gave her the figure, and she gasped "—and then thereafter you'll get a percentage of the royalties when the book is on the shelves. We would also like for you to do some publicity, signings and so forth; but that will be when the book is published. Tentatively we're scheduling it for next spring. Sound okay?"

"Oh, yes," she said, beaming. "Mr. Harris, I'm just overwhelmed. I don't know how to thank you."

"It's a good book," he replied. "We're proud to publish it. If the terms are okay with you, we're sending the contracts down by courier. If you could send us the single drawing by next week or the week after, that would be fine."

"Yes, I can do that," she agreed, without mentioning her condition. She gave him her street address, trying not to let Jared's black scowl unnerve her.

"We'll be in touch."

"Thanks again," she replied, and hung up.

"Who's Daniel Harris?" Jared demanded.

Her eyebrows levered up. "What business is it of yours?"

The scowl darkened. "You're living with an ex-mercenary and handing out your home address to strangers in New York."

"Well, I am getting to be quite the vamp, aren't I?" she asked, and blinked her long lashes at him.

His teeth set audibly. "Who is he?"

She just glared, but he didn't back down an inch.

"All right! He's an editor. I sold my children's book to him."

"Book?"

"The one I was working on? Lisa Parks's puppies?"

"Oh."

"They bought it. They're sending me a contract to sign."

"I'll have an attorney look it over for you," he offered.

She sat up. "Max isn't touching my book! Or my contracts!"

His expression lightened. "You're jealous."

She flushed. "So are you!"

He looked odd for a minute. He blinked. "Yes," he said finally.

That floored her. She just looked at him, dumbfounded.

"You might be carrying my child," he said after a minute, and something odd flashed in his eyes. "I'm territorial."

"It's my child, if there is one," she shot back. "You're not taking me over."

He was thinking, scheming, planning. It was in his expression. "I'm good at hostile takeovers."

"Remember me? The uncouth savage from Outer Cowpasture?" she prompted. "Imagine showing me off at cocktail parties! Think of the embarrassment when I open my mouth and drawl at your circle of friends."

"I don't have friends," he said coldly.

"Why not?"

He shrugged. "I never know if they're seeing me or my money."

"Fortunately I don't have that problem. Being poor has its advantages." She thought for a minute. "Well, I won't be as poor as I was, I suppose. If the book sells, I mean."

"If it's publicized enough, it will sell."

She gave him a wry look. "Don't even think about it. I can do my own publicity."

"I have a firm of publicists working for me, making up ad campaigns for the corporation and its divisions," he said.

"I don't work for your corporation."

"I thought we were family," he began.

"Tony and I are family. We just voted you out," she told him.

He moved closer to the bed. "You'd leave me alone in the world, with nobody?"

"You've got Max."

"I fired Max."

"I'm sure she won't be hard to replace," she said cattily. "And I'm sure you have a whole houseful of beautiful women ready to step into her shoes in other ways," she added meaningfully.

He avoided her eyes. "I'm a man," he said curtly. "Men have needs."

"Yes. I noticed," she said deliberately.

He moved restlessly. "I told you, I didn't mean for that to happen!"

She colored. "Great! If there's a baby, we can tell him he was an accident."

"Don't you dare!" he exploded.

She felt embarrassed at the statement, which she hadn't meant. He just made her mad. "I like babies," she said slowly, putting her hands flat on her stomach. "But it's scary, thinking about having one. They're so little . . ."

"When Ellen was born," he recalled quietly, "they put her in my arms. I'd never seen anything so tiny, so perfect." A sad smile touched his hard mouth. "I counted little fingers and toes, kissed her little nose, her feet. I never loved anything so much . . ."

He stopped and turned away, walking to the window. He looked out over the kitchen garden. It took him a minute to get his emotions under control.

Sara felt guilty. He'd loved his little child. He was afraid to have another one, afraid of losing it. He was closing up inside his shell for safety.

"Lisa and Cy lost their first baby," she said softly. "It was born with several rare birth defects. The doctors couldn't save it, and they had specialists all the way from Dallas. Lisa said it wasn't meant to be. They grieved for years. They were afraid to try again, too. But when she got pregnant again, everything went perfectly. She and Cy are like children themselves. They're crazy about this child and talking about having more. You can't hide from life," she concluded quietly. "I know. I've tried to. I have nightmares, remembering how my father died. I blocked it out for years, but sometimes now I can see it. I was conscious for just a few seconds after the concussion hit me. He was blown apart . . ." She had to stop. The memory was nightmarish.

He came back to the bed, standing over her. "I wish you could have told me about it," he said softly. "You haven't had it easy, have you?"

"Neither have you," she replied.

He drew in a slow breath. "I've lost my nerve," he said after a minute. "I don't think I could cope with losing another child."

"Neither did Lisa and Cy, but it didn't stop them from trying again. Life doesn't come with guarantees. Sometimes you just have to have faith."

"Faith," he scoffed. His face was hard, closed. "I hated God."

"He doesn't hate you," she said gently. "He doesn't punish people, you know. We have free choice. He doesn't control every second of our lives. Bad things happen. That's just the way life is. But faith is how we cope. Especially in small towns."

"You're only nineteen," he said quietly. "How did you come to be so wise, at such an age?"

"I had a hard life as a child," she replied simply. "It teaches you things you wouldn't learn in a protected environment." She searched his eyes. "I had a best friend at the mission in Africa. I watched her die of a fever. All the medicines we had couldn't cure her. One of our best workers, a nice boy named Ahmed, was gunned down two feet from his front door by rebels. He was smiling when he died. He said he was going to heaven now, and we weren't to grieve." She shook her head. "In Jacobsville, you can walk down the streets after dark and not get shot. I think of that as miraculous. People here just take it for granted."

He sat down beside her on the bed. "Where we sunk wells in South America," he said, "there were people living in conditions that you couldn't conceive of if you hadn't been there. Women were old by the age of forty, men were missing fingers, teeth, eyes. Children died in infancy of diseases we can prevent here. I felt guilty for making a profit from oil, when all those conditions were going on around me. I set up a foundation, to provide small grants to people who wanted to start businesses of their own. Women, mostly, who could weave cloth and keep chickens and a cow so they had eggs and milk and butter to sell. You'd be amazed at how far that little bit of money went."

She was fascinated. "But they sent kidnappers after you," she said.

He nodded. "The government nationalized all the oil companies. I pulled my people out. I'd already foiled one kidnapping attempt when I went down with our corporate attorneys to try to work the situation out. Do you know what a narco-terrorist is, Sara?"

"Yes. I've read about them. They grow coca and process it in factories on site, and sell coca paste to drug lords who market it in the U.S. and elsewhere," she said. "They control politicians."

"They always need money, for bribes and weapons," he said. "They've discovered that kidnapping wealthy foreigners is a quick, easy way to get cash. It's a bold move, sending people up here to try to nab me. But there was a raid just recently that cost them several million in operating cash. They thought I'd be easy to kidnap. Their mistake."

"Tony said that's why you came here," she replied. "A lot of his former comrades live in Jacobsville."

He nodded. "But it didn't work. They tracked me here without attracting attention. They might have succeeded, if you hadn't been canny enough to panic them." He shook his head, smiling softly down at her. "You're brave, Sara. I don't know a single other person, except maybe Tony, who'd have had the nerve to do what you did."

She felt warm inside. She shouldn't. He'd said terrible things to her. Besides, there was the possibility of a child. She looked up at him steadily. "So the kidnappers are in custody. Those worries are over. Right?"

His lips made a thin line. "They didn't actually kidnap anyone," he said. "Cash Grier is holding them right now on a weapons charge."

She felt her heart skip. "A weapons charge?"

"They had an AK-47 in the van and no permit," he replied. He frowned. "Actually I don't think you can get a permit for an automatic weapon as a private citizen. I'll have to ask Cash. Anyway, it's illegal in their case. But they didn't carry you out of the store or even lay hands on you." He sighed. "So there's a good chance that they're going to get out on bail as soon as their high-priced American attorney gets them to a bail hearing."

"The judge can set a high bail, if he or she is asked to," she began.

He smiled cynically. "Drug lords have so much money that even a million dollars is like pocket change to them. It won't help."

"But if they get out, won't they just try again?"

His expression changed. "Worried about me?" he asked in a soft, deep tone.

"I can worry, even if you're not family anymore," she returned pertly.

He laughed softly. The trap didn't feel like a trap. Maybe he'd been too grief-stricken to think of a child on his own, but this one had fallen right into his lap. Well, he'd helped it to, and he shouldn't feel happy about losing control with Sara, all the same.

She was watching his expression change, unable to follow what he was thinking. He seemed to be more comfortable with her now than he had several minutes ago. That didn't mean he was happy about their situation.

"What will you do?" she asked, because she really was worried.

"I don't know," he replied. "I think I'll go talk to the police chief." He frowned. "Now there's an odd bird," he said conversationally. "Someone said he was a Texas Ranger once."

"He was something else, once, too," she mused.

"The sniper thing?" he scoffed. "Gossip, I imagine."

"No," she said. "It's not. A Drug Enforcement Administration agent's little girl was kidnapped by the former head of one of the Mexican cartels last year. They threatened to kill her if the feds didn't back off their raid on a local drug warehouse. Cash Grier took out two of the kidnappers and the DEA agents got the rest and rescued the child. He made the shots in the dark from over six hundred yards away." She lowered her voice. "They say he was a covert assassin once."

His eyebrows lifted. "And he's a small town police chief?"

"He's happy here," she told him. "His wife, Tippy, used to be a model. They called her the 'Georgia Firefly.'"

"Well!"

"They have a little girl named Tris." She gave him a smirk. "So, you see, not everybody dislikes living in Outer Cowpasture."

"Touché," he replied.

"Maybe he has friends who could get those three guys on some sort of terrible federal charge," she murmured. "We never found out who the DEA agents were," she added. "One of them does undercover work, so he wasn't identified. The other, the child's mother, was a DEA agent, too. Her husband bought property here, but they're living in Houston until the end of the school year because of their daughter. They didn't want to put her into a strange school midyear."

"Do you know everything about everybody here?" he asked curiously.

"Sure," she told him. "Everybody does."

He glanced at the door, where Tony was just entering with soup and sandwiches on a tray. He glared at his ex-boss. "She needs to eat her lunch."

Jared got to his feet. "I was just leaving." He smiled down at Sara. "Eat it all up, like a good girl."

She flushed. "I'm not a kid."

He sighed. "Compared to me you are," he said quietly, and he looked lost.

"My mother was nineteen when she had me," Tony said abruptly.

Jared glanced at him, curious.

Tony shrugged. "It isn't the age, it's the mileage," he clarified, meeting the other man's eyes. "She's got almost as much mileage as you have. She just looks younger."

"I suppose so."

"I like babies," Tony said, setting the tray across Sara's legs.

Jared withdrew into his safe shell. He didn't say a word.

"Try not to get killed," Sara told him. "I'm in no condition to go to a funeral."

He laughed. "I'll do my best."

Tony glanced at him. "They'll try again," he said. "The minute they make bail, and they'll make it."

"Yes, I know," Jared replied. He pursed his lips. "I've had an idea."

"What?" Tony asked.

Jared glared. "Oh, sure, I tell you, and you tell her, and she tells everybody in Jacobsville."

"I only gossip about people I like," Sara protested.

"And pigs fly," he returned. "I'll come by tomorrow and check on you."

"I'll be fine," Sara protested.

He glanced at her belly with an unreadable expression. "I'll come by anyway."

He turned and left without another word.

"We could have offered him lunch," Sara told Tony. "Even if he isn't part of our family anymore."

"He'd curdle the milk," Tony muttered.

Sara laughed and finished her soup.

Jared went straight to Police Chief Cash Grier's office when he left Sara's house.

Cash was on the phone, but he hung up when Jared walked in and closed the office door.

"I haven't let them out yet," Cash told him, anticipating the reason he'd come.

"They'll skip town the minute they can make bail," Jared replied.

"In the old days, I'd have thrown them out the back door and charged them with attempted escape."

Jared glowered at him. "Civilization has its price."

Cash sighed. "Spoilsport."

Jared sat down in the visitor's chair without being

asked. "They'll be as much a danger to Sara as they are to me," he said. "We have to find a way to prove they're kidnappers."

Cash's dark eyebrows went up. "We could stuff you in their van under a blanket and catch them at the city limits sign," he suggested dryly.

Jared chuckled. "That's just what I had in mind."

"It would be entrapment, I'm afraid," Cash replied, leaning back in his chair. "We'll have to find a legal way to keep them locked up."

"Suppose we have Tony the Dancer arrested for breaking and entering?"

Cash blinked. "Are we having the same conversation?"

"You could put him in the cell with the three kidnappers," he continued. "Tony could offer to help them get me, for revenge."

Cash whistled. "And I thought I was the only dangerous person in town."

"I didn't inherit what I've got," Jared told him. "The first company I started was a security business. I hired my men and myself out to oil companies as protection against terrorist attacks. An elderly oil tycoon with no dependents took a liking to me, taught me the business and left his company to me when he died. Eventually I sold the security company and parlayed the oil business into a worldwide corporation."

"So that's how you know Tony the Dancer."

Jared nodded. "He was the first man I hired, in the

days before he worked for a legitimate authority. He still does odd jobs for me, from time to time."

Cash pursed his lips. "Then I suppose you know about his real background?"

Jared chuckled. "I check out everybody who works for me. His dossier was, to say the least, impressive."

"Yes, and how fortunate for him that he's not wanted in the States," Cash replied. "The only man I know who's a target for assassination in more countries than Tony is an undercover DEA agent named Ramirez."

"I know him," Jared said unexpectedly. "He worked for me, too, in the early days."

"He worked for a lot of people. He's involved in a case right now, so if you see him anywhere, pretend you don't know him."

"Isn't it risky for him to go undercover again?" Jared asked, curious.

"It is in Texas. He helped bring down the late drug lord, Manuel Lopez. But he's not known locally, except by a few of us with ties to mercenaries. His name was never mentioned when his partner's child was kidnapped by drug smugglers here last year."

"I understand you brought down some of the kidnappers."

Cash nodded. "Some skills never get rusty." He leaned forward. "Who talks to Tony, you or me?"

"It had probably better be you," Jared said heavily. "He'd enjoy cutting my throat right now because of Sara."

"You didn't put Sara in the hospital," Cash replied, misunderstanding.

"No, but I may have gotten her pregnant," he said uncomfortably.

Cash's good humor eclipsed. His black eyes flashed at the man across the desk.

"We're all capable of making ungodly mistakes," Jared said quietly. "I don't think I've ever been around an innocent in my whole life. In recent years, women are as aggressive as men when it comes to sex."

"Not all of them," Cash said in an icy tone. "And Sara's only nineteen."

"I didn't find that out until it was too late," he said. "She seems older than she is."

"Considering her past, that isn't surprising."

Jared nodded. "I didn't know about that, either." His eyes held a sad, faraway look. "My daughter died eight months ago," he said. "I've grieved until it was an effort just to get out of bed in the morning. I don't understand how, but Sara brought the sunlight back in for me. I never meant to hurt her."

"I'm sorry," Cash said. "I know what it is to lose a child."

Jared met his eyes. There was, suddenly, a bond between them, forged of grief.

"Tony seems very fond of Sara."

Jared's face hardened. "Well, I'll take care of that when the time comes. If she's pregnant, that's my child. No way is he raising it."

Cash's eyebrows arched.

Jared cleared his throat. "He's not going to be able to settle down, anyway."

"You need to meet a few people around town," Cash told him. "Starting with Eb Scott."

"Eb Scott lives here?" he exclaimed.

"Yes. He's got a state-of-the-art training center for military and government resources," he said. "A lot of ex-mercs work for him."

"I'd never have expected Scott to be able to settle down."

"Most people said the same about me," Cash replied, smiling. "I think it comes down to what's important to you. It used to be work, for me. Now it's Tippy and our baby. And Rory," he added. "My brother-in-law." He chuckled. "He's twelve years old."

"It's still work that gets the major portion of my time," Jared replied. "But just recently I've begun to wonder if I don't have my priorities skewed." He studied his boots. "There aren't many women around like Sara. Of course, she's years too young for me."

"Judd Dunn, my assistant chief, is married to a young woman who was twenty-one at the same time he was thirty-two. They have twins and they're very happy. It depends a great deal on the woman. Some mature sooner than others."

"I guess they do."

Cash got to his feet. "I think I'll go have a word with Tony."

"I think I'll stop by the flower shop and start working on my campaign."

"Campaign?"

"Tony's not marrying Sara," Jared said shortly.

"That would be her decision," Cash cautioned.

"Yes, well, he can't afford as many roses and chocolates as I can, so let's see him compete!"

Cash knew when to shut up.

Sara was curious to see Cash Grier at her door. It must have something to do with the would-be kidnappers, she thought.

"How's it going, Sara?" he asked, smiling. "Feeling better?"

"A lot, thanks. Why are you here?"

"I have to talk to Tony." He moved closer to the bed. "You wouldn't mind having someone else stay with you for a couple of days, would you?"

"Why would you ask that?"

"Well, I'm going to have to arrest Tony for breaking and entering," he began, "and I don't want you to be here alone."

"Arrest . . . ?"

"Now, calm down," he said. "It isn't for real."

"What isn't for real?" Tony asked, carrying two cups of coffee. "We can talk in the living room," he told Cash. "Sara, will you be okay for a few minutes?"

She couldn't put two words together.

Cash put his finger to his lips, walked out with Tony and closed the door, leaving Sara worried and quiet.

"But I didn't do it to steal anything," Tony was protesting. "I had to feed the cat!"

"It isn't for real," Cash insisted. "We want you to have to be thrown in with the kidnappers. Jared's having you arrested. You're furious at him. You want to get back at him. They'd love to help, I'm sure."

Tony put his coffee cup down. "Okay, now, you're starting to scare me. Have you been drinking?"

Cash chuckled. "Not today." He leaned forward. "Here's the deal. I have to turn the men loose. All I'm holding them on is a weapons charge. I can't convince a sane judge to set a million dollars bail for a weapons charge. They're going to skip town the minute the cell door opens. If they do, they may try to grab Sara again, or they may go after Jared. Either way, it's going to lead to tragedy."

Tony pursed his lips. "Oh. I get it. You want me to lead them into a trap so that you can charge them with kidnapping."

"That's exactly what I want."

Tony's eyes narrowed. "Jared put you up to it."

"He did," Cash confessed. "He's worried about Sara."

"Not enough to keep himself from seducing her," Tony said angrily.

"I heard about that, too. He's sorry he did it. But if you have plans to help her raise the baby—if there is a baby—you're in for the fight of your life," he added. "He's just starting to feel possessive about her."

Tony scoffed. "He goes through women like a sword through tissue paper," he said coldly.

"Like a man who's afraid to risk his heart twice, I would have thought," Cash replied solemnly. "He told me about his little girl."

Tony's hard demeanor softened. "Yeah. That was rough. She was a sweet kid. He didn't spend nearly enough time with her, but he loved her. She loved him, too. Hell of a tragedy."

"Let's not have another one," Cash said. "Help me get these guys off the street before they do something stupid. Sara might not be so lucky a second time. And they wouldn't hesitate to kill her, after she foiled their plan so deftly."

"I thought about that, myself."

"It's only going to be for a couple of days," Cash said, "but we need somebody to stay with Sara. I thought maybe Harley Fowler . . ."

Tony's dark eyes twinkled. "Did you? I was thinking that Jared might be willing to sacrifice himself."

"Let him stay with Sara?"

Tony nodded. "It might be just the thing to get them both to sort out their priorities. And you could have extra patrols on the house, too. Just in case."

Cash grinned. "I like the way you think."

Tony just chuckled.

If making the decision was easy, telling it to Sara wasn't.

She looked utterly tragic. "But you can't put Tony

in jail!" she cried. "I thought you were my friend!"

Cash grimaced. Tony was standing beside him in handcuffs.

"It isn't what you think, Sara," Tony agreed.

"Jared Cameron put you up to it, didn't he?" she demanded, and Tony grimaced, too.

She was almost in tears when the front door opened and Jared walked in carrying a suitcase. Sara spotted him, picked up a vase on the bedside table, drew back and flung it at him past the two stunned men. It shattered near Jared's shoulder.

"You get out of my house!" she yelled.

Cash looked at Tony. "Are you sure asking him to stay with her is a good idea?" he asked.

Eleven

Jared managed to look disgusted. "Is that any way to treat the father of your child?" he demanded.

"I'm not having a child!" she yelled, red-faced.

"How do you know?" he retorted. "It's too early for a pregnancy test."

"He's got you there," Cash interjected.

"You shouldn't be getting so upset, Sara, it's not good for you," Tony said worriedly.

"He's absolutely right," Jared said, putting down the suitcase. "I'm going to take care of you while Tony's away."

"You make it sound like he's going on vacation," Sara muttered. "He's going to jail!"

"Yes, I know."

She frowned. "You know?" She looked from him, to Tony, to Cash Grier. She wasn't stupid. "Oh."

"It's the only way," Tony told her. "Otherwise, you'll never be out of danger."

"You're sure you aren't going to keep him?" she asked Cash.

Cash smiled. "I'm sure. We'd better get going."

"I'll be back before you know it," Tony told Sara. He paused beside Jared. "You be careful, too. There may only be three of them, or there may not."

"I know that, too," Jared replied. He smiled wryly. "Don't forget who taught you surveillance techniques."

Tony chuckled. "I wouldn't dare. See you, Sara."

"See you, Tony."

Cash nodded and walked him out the door.

Jared watched them leave, his hands deep in his pockets.

"What did you mean about surveillance techniques?" she asked.

He turned. His green eyes were mischievous. "The first business I ever owned provided private security. Tony and I worked together until we could train assistants."

She studied him quietly. "And what did you do before that?" she asked.

"I was a cop in San Antonio."

Her lips fell open. "For heaven's sake! And you own an oil corporation now?"

"I've had a lot of help along the way. Most of it from Tony," he told her, stepping gingerly around shattered pottery. "We were always best friends until you came along."

"Well, you know why that happened," she muttered.

"Yes, I do. No need to remind me." He accidentally stood on a piece of ceramic that broke again. "Where's a broom?"

"In the closet in the kitchen," she began, but he was gone before she could ask anything else.

He came back with a broom and a dustpan and cleaned the floor as naturally as if he'd done it all his life.

"Were you in the military, before you were a policeman?" she asked, curious about him.

"Army," he said. "I was in special forces. So was Tony." He poured the broken pieces of what had been a vase into a nearby trash can and propped the broom and dustpan beside it. "He was best man at my wedding."

He'd never talked to her like this before. It was fascinating. "Did you love your wife?"

"Yes, when I married her," he said. "We both came from ranch families. My father got kicked in the head by a bull and died soon afterward. My mother grieved herself to death. Marian's parents died in a tornado outbreak. We'd known each other most of our lives. We were friends. I suppose we thought friendship was enough. It wasn't."

"Why did she leave you?"

"She found someone she loved," he said simply. "She took our daughter, Ellen, with her. She was a wonderful mother. Ellen was happy with her. I wasn't home much, but when I was, Ellen was always welcome to come and stay with me. My permanent home is in Oklahoma," he added, "where my corporation headquarters is."

"But you bought a ranch here," she said, mystified.

"I told you at the cemetery that I needed a change," he said. "I meant it. I was grieving for Ellen and upset over Marian's suicide just afterward. I thought new surroundings would help me get past the depression."

"The surroundings don't matter much," Sara said gently. "Pain and grief are portable. They go with you."

He glanced down at her and smiled warmly. "There's that odd insight again. You really are old for your age."

"And getting older by the day," she replied.

He moved to the bed and sat down beside her. He was wearing jeans and a chambray shirt, open at the neck. He looked very sensual with his hair faintly ruffled and his nice tan.

Without warning, his big, lean hand pressed gently on her flat stomach. "I made a hell of a fuss about it. But maybe it wouldn't be a bad thing, if you're pregnant. I'll be a better father this time around."

"You can come and visit anytime you like," she told him.

He frowned. "My child isn't being born out of wed-lock."

"Well, he won't have much choice, because I am not marrying you," she said firmly.

"Why not?" he asked, and seemed really intent on her reason.

She colored and averted her eyes. "Because I don't ever want to have to do that again."

He lost color. He knew his heart had stopped. "Sara, it was your first time and I was in too much of a hurry," he said softly. "I hurt you because I rushed it."

Her face was red by now. She couldn't possibly look at him. She clasped her hands together and picked at her thumbnail nervously.

He tilted her embarrassed face up to his. "I won't ever hurt you again," he promised. "It gets better. Honest."

She grimaced.

She was so young, he thought sadly. Probably he should never have touched her. But she made him feel young and vital and full of fire. She brought feelings of nurturing and possession to him. He'd never wanted a woman for keeps. Even his wife had been a footnote in his life. But this woman was magic. Sheer magic.

He thought back to their first meeting, and inspiration struck. "You could have your own bookstore," he said.

Her eyes widened. "My own . . . ?"

"We could even build a child activity center into it.

The baby could play while you worked. And if customers with children came in, they could play there while their parents browsed. There could be a snack shop with fancy coffee."

She was melting. Just the thought of her own place was tantalizing. "Really?"

He smiled at her enthusiasm. She couldn't even hide it. "I could delegate more, and travel less. We could have more than one child."

She looked into his eyes with all her longings showing there. Children. A home. A business. Max. She scowled and glared at him.

"What?"

"Are you sure you fired Max?" she wondered aloud. "Tony says you're always firing her, but she always comes back."

"This time it's permanent," he assured her. He drew in a long breath. "I'm through with the playboy life as well. I thought a few encounters would be a cure for loneliness. It wasn't. It only made me feel cheap."

That was a powerful admission, she thought. And he did seem sincere.

His big hand pressed gently against her stomach. He looked at it, his eyes quiet and full of wonder. "You know your body better than I do. What's your gut feeling?"

"I . . . I don't know," she faltered. "Really. It's too soon."

He smiled. "Well, either way, we'll cope. If you aren't pregnant, we'll spend some time getting to know each other before we start a family. We'll have plenty of time." He pursed his lips. "And Tony will have to find himself a new source of entertainment, besides looking after you and cooking," he said, and felt guilty and elated all at once. If she really was pregnant, Tony was right out of the running as a potential husband.

She frowned. "Tony will be all right, won't he? There are three of those men. They're all big and muscular, and they can't watch them all the time while they're in custody at the county detention center." Which was where they would be taken, because the city didn't maintain a jail.

He chuckled. "I've seen Tony take on six guys and walk away grinning," he told her. "It's the best idea we could come up with," he added, tugging the sheet up over her belly tenderly. "We can't risk having them make bail and come after you again."

She grimaced. "Life used to be so uncomplicated until you came along," she sighed wistfully.

"You're too young to appreciate monotony," he returned. He bent and kissed her gently on the forehead. "Try to get some sleep. I have a few phone calls to make, then we'll talk some more about the future."

She could have argued that there might not be one, but it was sweet to pretend. She smiled at him and agreed.

Tony was muttering, furious, as he was put into the general quarters in detention, wearing an orange jumpsuit and flip-flops. He glowered at everybody around him.

"I didn't even take anything!" he yelled at the guard who'd delivered him. "I was just feeding the cat."

"Tell it to a judge," the deputy replied wearily.

"You bet I will!" he raged. "He just wants me out of the way, so he can walk off with my girl. You tell Jared Cameron that when I get out of here, I'm going to drive a truck over him!"

"Terroristic threats and acts carry a felony charge," the amused deputy called over his shoulder.

Tony gave him a four-fingered salute.

One of the men in the dormitory was giving him odd looks. Tony stared at him belligerently. "You got a problem?" he demanded.

The man was about his own age, tall and muscular, with a mustache and tattoos over both arms. "Sounds like you got one," he said with a hint of a foreign accent. "Somebody locked you up for nothing, huh?"

Tony moved to a chair and sat down. "Something like that."

The man took a chair beside him. "Jared Cameron? I think I heard of him."

"Most people have," Tony muttered. "God, I wish I had a smoke!"

"Can't have cigarettes in here, my friend," the other man chuckled. "But I could get you some weed, if you got anything to trade."

"Do I look like I got anything to trade?" Tony demanded. "What are you in here for?"

"Weapons charge," the man said easily. "But me and my boys, we'll be out as soon as we have our bail hearing."

"Lucky you," Tony told him. "I'm in for breaking and entering. It's a felony."

"Not a big one," his companion said.

Tony stared at him. "It is if you're out on probation," he said.

The man grimaced. "Ah. I see. Too bad."

"Yeah. Too bad." His eyes narrowed angrily. "Jared Cameron better hope I get the death penalty for it, because the day I get out of here, he's a dead man. I know his routine, the layout of his house, everything!"

"How is that?"

"I was working as his bodyguard," Tony scoffed, "until he took a fancy to my girl and stole her from me. Now he wants me out of the way."

The man looked down at the floor. The room smelled of foul odors. Tony wondered if any of these people had ever been introduced to soap. One was obviously coming down from a drug-induced high, shaking and threatening people. Another was staggering drunk. Nobody looked as if he was a stranger to the criminal justice system.

"You know," the other man began casually, "you could make a lot of money and get even with Cameron at the same time if you wanted to."

Tony was all ears. "I could? How?"

"I know some people who would pay a lot of money for him."

"He's no pushover," Tony warned.

"Yes, but he is now lacking his bodyguard," the man persisted. "Before he can hire another one, it would be a good time to apprehend him."

Tony stared at the man. "Yeah. It would, wouldn't it?"

The man got up. "I got to talk to my friends about it. But I think I could get you in on it, if you're interested."

"I got no money for a lawyer and Cameron didn't even offer to help me," Tony muttered. "In fact, I think it was him who told the police I broke into the girl's house. Some boss!"

The other man was grinning now. "You want to get even, yes?"

"Yes."

"We will talk more later."

Tony shrugged. "Well, I'm not going anywhere. Not right away, at least."

That night, the jailer came and took Tony out, mumbling something about an attorney wanting to talk to him about his arrest.

Cash Grier was waiting in the interrogation room. He turned as Tony was escorted inside and the door closed, with the guard standing on the other side of it.

"Any luck?" Cash asked him.

Tony grinned. "Their ringleader wants me to help them put the snatch on Jared. He's been talking his two companions into it. One of them thinks I'm a plant. The other has, basically, the IQ of a plant."

Cash chuckled. "So you're in?"

"Seems so. I expect them to double-cross me the instant they see Jared in their sights, of course."

Cash thought for a minute. "We'll have Sara call a bail bondsman for you. We'll pay him without letting anyone else know. When you and the three outlaws get out, we'll have you wired and a homing device placed in their van. As soon as they grab Jared, we'll have them for attempted kidnapping and give them to the feds."

"Not a bad plan."

"You really think so? Thanks," Cash said with enthusiasm. "I don't actually know any feds, you understand, but I can look them up in the phone book."

Tony was laughing. "And they give you real bullets, do they?"

"I haven't shot anybody in a year, at least," Cash said with mock dismay.

"Just don't shoot me, when you show up to get those other guys. I weigh five pounds more than I should because of bullets they can't take out."

"I have a couple of my own that never left," Cash replied. "Okay. I'll go. I'll talk to Jared and have a couple of my officers standing by. Don't do anything until they actually have Jared in their van," he added cautiously. "We have to have charges that will stick."

"You keep an eye on Sara as well," Tony told him.

"These guys don't act like they're hitting on all six cylinders. There's no telling what they may try next."

"I noticed. You know," he added seriously, "you look pretty good in orange."

Tony's eyes narrowed. "No fair picking on innocent victims of crime."

"Oh, that's rich, coming from you," Cash chuckled. "I'm leaving."

"Tell Sara not to worry about me."

"I can tell her, but it won't do any good. She likes you."

He shrugged. "I like her, too."

"We'll find a way to separate you from the kidnappers at the bail hearing so we can get you wired. I've already done their van."

"They may look for a homing device," Tony pointed out.

"They can look all they like," he replied. "They'll never find this one. See you."

"Yeah. You, too."

It was a very good plan. Tony was wired just before he left with the three men, now dressed again in their civilian clothing as Tony was. They seemed to trust him.

But once they were in the van, the driver spoke in an Arab dialect on his cell phone, blissfully unaware that Tony spoke that particular dialect.

The leader of the kidnappers told his contact that they were on their way to get the woman Jared loved.

Somehow they'd found out that Jared was staying with Sara. They were going to hold her long enough to make him give himself up to them, then they were going to kill her. They would kill Tony, too, because he could become a liability once the girl was dead. They would kill Jared eventually, the minute they had the ransom in their hands. They already had airplane tickets. It would be a matter of hours. The contact could meet them at the airport in Belize where they usually hooked up.

Tony cursed the change of plans. He couldn't warn anybody. If he repeated what the kidnapper had said, they'd know he spoke Arabic and he'd be dead. If he didn't, Sara would be in terrible danger. Jared was with her. It would be an easy matter to take both of them.

He had to pretend that he hadn't understood a word and act nonchalant. "Don't you guys kill Cameron," he cautioned belligerently. "He's all mine!"

"Be assured, we have no plans to kill him. We only wish for the ransom he will bring." He told the driver to slow down as they approached Sara's house.

"Hey," Tony murmured, looking out the windshield. "That ain't Cameron's house!"

"He isn't in his house," the leader of the three men replied. "Cameron is with your girlfriend."

"Don't you hurt her," Tony warned.

"Relax, my friend!" the other man laughed. "We intend only to take Cameron hostage. Then you and the girl will be free. I give you my word."

Which was as good as his sense of fashion, Tony thought sarcastically, but he only nodded and pretended to believe the man. While he was nodding, he was considering his options. He was not only wearing a wire, he had a hidden gun in an ankle holster and a commando knife in a sheath inside his slacks. He had a watch with a pull-out garrote. All that, combined with advanced martial arts training, should stand him in good stead if he had the opportunity to act.

"You taking Cameron out of the country after you nab him?" Tony asked.

The three men were intent on the sparse lighting of the small house just ahead. "Yes, yes," the leader said, distracted. "We have a base in Peru, where we can hold him until the ransom is paid."

Tony doubted that Jared Cameron would be alive after the ransom was in their hands.

"Stop!" the leader told the driver. "You stay and wait for our signal," he added. "We will take the bodyguard with us. Be vigilant."

"Of course," the driver replied.

The leader slid open the side panel of the van and motioned the shorter man and Tony out behind him.

"You will go first," he told Tony. "Knock on the door and pretend that you have come to check on the woman."

"Not a bad plan," Tony said, grinning, because this plan would give him room to act. "You guys are smart."

"You must not harm Cameron," the leader told him

firmly. "We need the ransom very badly. Later, we will give him to you, once we have the funds."

Tony pretended to mull over the suggestion. "Okay. But you better give me a crack at him."

"We will. Of course we will," the leader said. He was now holding an automatic weapon. So was his companion.

It was going to be tricky, Tony mused, but he'd been in tighter spots. "You guys better get out of sight," Tony told them, hoping Cash Grier was listening closely to what he said to the hidden microphone.

"We will be just around this corner," the leader said. His face went hard. "We will have you in our sights, also. For insurance."

"In other words, I get shot if I try anything funny," Tony replied. "Hell, I want the guy as much as you do!"

The leader seemed to relax, a little. "Very well." He motioned to the second man and they went, light on their feet, around the corner of the porch.

Tony knocked on the door. He heard footsteps coming. They weren't Jared's footsteps. He would have known them anywhere. He had to hide a grin.

The door opened. Tony dived through it as Cash Grier slammed the door. Outside there was gunfire.

"Quick reflexes," Cash remarked to Tony.

"I've, uh, had a little practice over the years. How about Jared and Sara?"

"When we heard your plan over the wire," Cash

replied, "we got them out of the house. They're at Jared's. Nobody here but old Morris the cat, and we put him in a closet, just in case."

The shooting ended.

"All clear!" a voice called.

Cash and Tony went out onto the porch, where four Jacobsville police officers and a man in a suit were leading the two would-be kidnappers toward the front door. In the yard, the wheel man was standing in front of his van, handcuffed, with two other men in suits holding guns on him.

"Nice operation," Cash told his men. "I knew that extra training in hostage negotiation would come in handy."

"Hostage negotiation?" Tony exclaimed. "They've all got guns!"

Cash looked sheepish. "Well, you negotiate your way and I'll negotiate my way."

The officers chuckled. So did Tony.

They had tape of the kidnappers confessing. Federal marshals were escorting them to Dallas, where they'd face federal charges. Their kidnapping days were over.

Tony was back at the ranch the next day, but Jared was sending him on to Oklahoma to make sure the house was ready for occupants. And also to make sure no more would-be kidnappers were lurking around.

"You take care, Sara," Tony told her gently, and

bent to kiss her on the cheek. "I expect we'll see each other again."

"I hope so." She hugged the big man and kissed his lean cheek. "Thanks for everything."

"No problem."

He shook hands with Jared. "I'll put Fred and Mabel to work getting the house set to rights. I assume you're not coming home alone," he added with a grin.

"You assume right," Jared said with a tender, possessive look toward Sara, who was just going back inside the house to make sure old Morris was all right. Tony had brought him over after all the excitement was past.

Tony stuck his hands in his pockets. "I've got to go back to my day job," he said. "I'm tempted to give it up, but it's comfortable."

"You're too young to want to be comfortable," Jared replied. "Besides, you have to keep those reflexes honed." He smiled mischievously. "You might be the next target for kidnappers looking for ransom." He looked past Tony at the sleek Jaguar sports car that had been lodging in the huge garage with Jared's classic automobiles. "That car could get you some unwelcome attention."

"You're just saying that because you don't want me to take it away," Tony shot back.

"You could always get a newer one," Jared suggested.

"I don't like the newer ones. I like that one."

"Damn!"

"Listen, we signed papers," Tony reminded him. "It isn't as if I stole it."

Jared pursed his lips. "There's a thought," he began.

Tony wagged a finger at him. "You report this car stolen, and you'll never make it home to Oklahoma without being arrested for possession of at least one Schedule I substance. I swear!"

"All right, all right," Jared muttered. "You did see it first at the auto show."

"Damned straight, I did." He hesitated. "You take care of yourself. And if there is a baby," he added, "I get to be the godfather."

Jared opened his mouth to speak.

"I know at least one shaman who can do nasty spells back home in North Carolina," he interrupted.

"You're from Georgia," he shot back.

"My foster parents are from Georgia. I was born in Cherokee, North Carolina."

"Yes, but your real father wasn't."

Tony gave him a glare. "We don't talk about him."

"You need to," Jared said solemnly. "You have to deal with it one day."

"I'm going to Oklahoma." Tony put his sunglasses on. "Right now."

"Nice shades."

"That's what my boss said."

"You didn't! You wouldn't swipe his sunglasses . . . ?"

"Of course I didn't swipe them. I won them."

"How?"

"He had a full house, I had four aces," he said smugly. "He threw the deck at me and walked out."

"Serves him right for getting suckered into playing poker with you," Jared said. He held out a hand. "Be safe."

Tony shook it. "You, too. I'll be in touch."

Sara came back with Morris in her arms, just in time to watch him drive away in a classic red sports car which, Jared told her, belonged to Tony.

"If Tony's leaving, why am I still here?" she asked Jared worriedly. "The bad guys are in Dallas by now, and I'm very fit."

He drew her to him, quiet and somber. "You're still here because we have things to talk about."

"Such as?"

He was oddly hesitant. "Come here."

He picked her up, Morris and all, and carried her into the living room, dropping down onto the sofa with her. Morris, uncomfortable, jumped down and went in search of food.

"We haven't known each other for a long time," Jared began quietly. "But I think we're basically the same sort of people. You're no doormat, and you're smart. You'd fit right in back in Oklahoma. Most of my friends are working people, just as I used to be. I don't travel in high social circles. In the past I spent a lot of time on airplanes, but that's going to stop. Whether or not you're pregnant doesn't matter right now. I'm going to delegate authority and start living my life for something other than making money."

"That sounds serious," she said, and her heart was hammering away in her chest. His eyes held a warmth she hadn't seen there before.

"It's very serious. I'm a good deal older than you," he began, "and I've had, and lost, a family. You could stay here and marry someone younger. Harley Fowler, maybe."

"I don't love Harley," she said softly, searching his eyes. "He's my friend. As for our ages," she added, "I'm more mature than a lot of women, because of what I've gone through."

He traced her mouth with a long forefinger. "Yes, you are," he agreed quietly. "Which leads to the next question."

"Which is?" she probed.

"Will you marry me, Sara?"

Twelve

Sara just looked at him, with her heart plain in her eyes. "Do you love me?" she asked, hesitating.

He smiled tenderly. "Yes," he said. "Of course I love you." He hesitated. His dark eyebrows lifted. "Well?"

"I loved you the minute you walked into the bookstore," she replied breathlessly. "I didn't really think you were an ogre, you know."

"Maybe I was, sort of," he returned, smiling. "But you've reformed me. So what do you think about getting married here and moving back to Oklahoma?"

"I don't mind where we live, as long as we're together," she told him. "But Morris the cat has to come with us." She paused. "Do you have pets?"

He laughed. "Do I! I've got saddle horses, cattle dogs, two huge Persian cats, an emu and an Amazon parrot."

"Oh, goodness," she exclaimed. "Why do you have an emu?"

He traced her mouth. "Ellen wanted one," he said simply. "I'd never even seen an emu, but a rancher I know was experimenting with them. We got Ellen a baby emu. She was crazy about him. We named him Paterson, after the Australian poet, and raised him with two border collies. The collies chase cattle, and the emu runs right along with them." He laughed. "It's quite a sight."

"I imagine so."

"We'll have cat furniture set up for Morris. After a few days of being spoiled, he'll adjust."

"What about your cats?"

He shrugged. "They'll all spit and fuss for a week, then they'll curl up and sleep together at night."

She smiled. It was usually the case when two sets of cats met. "We could be married here?" she asked, still having trouble believing it.

"Of course."

"I could wear a wedding gown, and carry a bouquet?"

"You can even have a photographer," he replied. "So that we have nice pictures to prove that we're married."

"That would be nice."

"We'll fly up to Dallas. You can have a gown from Neiman Marcus."

"I could buy something off the rack," she protested.

He brought her small hand to his lips and kissed the palm. "I'm fairly notorious," he said. "There will be news coverage. You wouldn't want me to look like a cheapskate on national television, would you?" he asked reasonably.

She laughed. "Nobody would think such a thing."

"Ha!"

Her head was spinning. She couldn't believe how quickly it had all happened. But there was that other thing, that worrisome thing . . .

He was watching her expression closely. He knew what the problem was. They were alone in the house. Old Morris had wandered off into the kitchen. He was safely established, for the time being. He pursed his lips as he looked down into Sara's worried face.

"There's no time like the present," he murmured.

"Excuse me?"

He bent and drew his mouth tenderly against Sara's. "Don't think," he whispered. "Don't worry. Just let go."

While he was talking, his hands were moving over her in soft, light caresses that made her mind over-load. She wanted to tell him something, but he'd unbuttoned her shirt and his mouth was already on her breasts.

She gasped at the sensations. They weren't like last

time. He was insistent, and expert. As the heated minutes sped past, she was as frantic to get her clothes out of the way as she had been to escape him the last time he'd touched her this way. But the sensations she was feeling now were explosive, overwhelming. She arched up to his ardent mouth and sobbed as his hands found her under the concealing cloth and created exquisite waves of pleasure.

She was under him. She felt the cold leather under her bare back, the heated weight of his body over and against hers. His mouth trailed down her body and back up again, in soft, arousing kisses that trespassed in all sorts of forbidden areas.

He asked her something, but she was already too far gone to hear him. Shivering, aching for satisfaction, she drew her legs up to ease his path, she arched up to his devouring mouth. It was the closest to heaven she'd ever imagined.

When she finally felt him, there, she dug her nails into his hips and held on for dear life as he buffeted her on the sofa. She was aware of the ceiling overhead, and the sound of his rough breathing, of her own frantic little gasps, as the pleasure began to build.

It was like climbing, she thought breathlessly, from one level to the next and the next and the next, and the pleasure increased with every fierce downward motion of his hips. She was dying. She couldn't survive. The pleasure was so deep and throbbing that it was almost pain. She strained for some goal she couldn't quite reach, her hips darting up to meet his, her body arched in a strained posture that was painful. She was almost there, almost there, almost . . . there!

He pushed down, hard, and she felt the world drop out from under her as a wave of white-hot pleasure racked her slender body and held her, motionless, in its vise-grip.

He lifted his head seconds later, drenched in sweat and barely able to get a whole breath. She was shivering in the aftermath. Her soft eyes were drowned in tears of joy as she lay under him, satiated.

"Now do you understand what was missing, the last time?" he whispered tenderly.

"Oh, yes." She locked her arms around his neck. She was trembling. "Is it always like this?"

"No," he murmured, smiling as his hips began to move again. "It gets better."

"You're kidding . . . !"

It was the last remark she was able to make for some time.

The wedding was beautiful, Sara thought, amazed at the media that gathered to watch Jared Cameron merge his oil empire with an unknown little bookseller in Jacobsville, Texas. One of the newswomen just shook her head, having covered stories that Jared featured in years ago. This little retiring Texas rose didn't seem at all the type of woman he'd marry. But then he looked down at his new bride, under her veil, and the look they exchanged made everything clear.

Love, the reporter thought, was truly an equalizer.

Harley Fowler congratulated them with a bitter-sweet smile. Sara hugged him and thanked him for all he'd done, especially scaring away the kidnappers in the bookstore. He wished them well. Sara was very fond of him, but she'd never felt romantic toward him. He knew it, and accepted it.

All the mercs showed up at the wedding, along with just about everybody in town. Sara felt like Cinderella at the ball. And now she was going away with her very own version of Prince Charming. She'd never been so happy.

Several days later, Sara had packed up everything, including Morris the cat, and Tony had arranged for Sara's possessions, plus Morris, to travel to the house in Oklahoma City, where Jared lived most of the time. Morris rode in a chauffeured limousine, with one of Tony's old comrades, and Jared's new body-guard, Clayton, at his side.

"Morris will never get over that," Sara told her new husband.

"It was the safest way I could think of," Jared replied, smiling. "Clayton will take great care of him. Tony trained him. He's good."

"We won't have to worry about kidnappers again, will we?" she worried.

He drew her gently into his arms. "*We* won't worry. We'll let Clayton worry. That's what he gets paid for."

"I thought Tony worked for you all the time," she commented.

"He was borrowed, for this assignment," he told her, and didn't offer any further information.

"He's rather mysterious, in his way," she said.

Jared raised an eyebrow. "You have no idea how mysterious," he assured her.

"Tell me."

He chuckled. "Not now. We've got work to do. You have to help me pack, now that we've got you covered."

"I'll miss Jacobsville," she said.

"I know you will, honey," he replied. "But you'll get used to it. Life has to be lived. You can't sit by the road and watch it pass."

"Maybe when we're old," she began.

He nodded. "Yes. Maybe when we're old."

"It was sweet of Dee to give us those rare World War II memoirs for a wedding present, wasn't it?" she asked.

"Yes, it was. And sweet of you to pack up all your grandfather's collection to bring with us. I'll only read one a week, I promise," he said when he saw her expression.

She frowned. "That reminds me, are you a sports fan?"

"I love soccer," he replied.

She beamed. "It's my favorite sport!"

"In that case, we'll make plans to go to the next World Cup."

"We could? Really?"

"Yes." He drew her against him and kissed her. "I love you."

She smiled. "I love you back."

"No regrets?"

She shook her head. "I'm going to take very good care of you."

He kissed her eyes closed. "And I'm going to take very good care of you." He rocked her in his arms. "Just for the record, any unusual nausea?"

She drew back and looked up at him, grimacing. "I'm afraid not. In fact, something monthly started up this morning. I'm sorry."

He kissed her. "We won't rush things," he said gently. "We'll grow together before we start a family. We'll travel. We'll go shopping. We'll find a nice location for a bookstore."

"You meant that?" she exclaimed.

"Of course I meant it," he said, smiling. "You can have anything you want, Sara."

She moved into his arms and pressed close. "Most of all, I want you, for all my life. I love you very much."

He swallowed hard and his arms closed around her. Grief had almost destroyed him, but this sweet, gentle woman had brought him back into the sunlight. She was his world now. He rested his cheek on her soft hair. "I love you, too, baby. I'll make you happy and keep you safe, all my life," he promised.

And he did.

Center Point Publishing

600 Brooks Road ● PO Box 1
Thorndike ME 04986-0001 USA

(207) 568-3717

US & Canada:
1 800 929-9108
www.centerpointlargeprint.com